FACES OF

VILLAIN

ZACHARY YAPLE

Matador
9 Priory Business Park,
Wistow Road, Kibworth Beauchamp,
Leicestershire. LE8 0RX
Tel: 0116 279 2299
Email: books@troubador.co.uk
Web: www.troubador.co.uk/matador
Twitter: @matadorbooks

ISBN 978 1838591 816

British Library Cataloguing in Publication Data.
A catalogue record for this book is available from the British Library.

Printed and bound in the UK by TJ International, Padstow, Cornwall
Typeset in 11pt Minion Pro by Troubador Publishing Ltd, Leicester, UK

Matador is an imprint of Troubador Publishing Ltd

For the book-reading pub crawlers, the petty-thieving shoplifters, the binge-drinking alcoholics, the poetic bantering lyricists, or those that love British satire... I hope you get something from this.

Shanty I

♠

The Public House

I N THE WET AND DIRTY STREETS OF SPITALFIELDS, LONDON, classes of the lowest gentry were homeless by the hundreds. The essence of poverty city 'twas rather crude and elementary; many creatures of all sorts roamed around in the plenty. Through them streets did them rats gnaw through salt, sand and debris. Eating all that was necessary, one could say 'twas a peasant's feast. The citizens of the poor grew to adore all the rats and whores running in and out of doors. They choose to ignore all faeces thrown from the upper floors; those were the days of eighteenth-century pub culture.

In that local pub, the Black Lyon's Den, did men banter and drink plenty of gin. And, just then, did Jack Trade walk through the entrance of the pub, that he'd grown accustomed to. All those punters who'd cheer and cry the name of a man would be recognized. A name most likely to be associated with scruples of thievery. 'Gentleman Jack', also known as 'Jack the Lad', was a cheeky champ (who could use a smack). A cheeky bugger, no less, who was well accepted in them days of greed and deception.

The owner of the Den was Ms Elizabeth Lyon. When she was young she frequently sold herself, now she was idle, sitting idly on the shelf. Retired from a life of debauchery, she was once admired by the disdainful poverty. Yet she did not give up the game one hundred percent; she hired younger women to pay for the rent. Girls as young as sixteen years old played a dirty little role in the Den's untold. One of whom had been used by all, black and bruised from the weekly drunken brawl. She was a hard nut to crack, especially for her man, *Monsieur Gentilhomme Jacques*.

Once in a while, we take a little visit to the Lyon's Den to indulge in the prohibited. At me side, those two lassies, that be Ms Eliabeth Lyon and Black-eyed Sally; the latter was the hard nut who we'd not bothered to tally. For she was a simpleton, a sod and a cretin, treated like a queen to be bruised and beaten. 'Tis why we all called her Black-eyed Sally; she had no shame in the darkest alleys. Yet she was our lover, and we took her under our wing, truly cared for her soul; she was our darlin'. We never did beat her, yet she was always bloody and bruised; 'tis why we call her this cruel nickname for the unseen abuse.

A song to hear, a voice to sing, round to the pub for a pint to drink. All of these activities involve the senses. A story is the only form of entertainment that strips away these contemplations, yet retains the conceptual part of one's deprived mind and ones starving heart.

A regular guest of the Lion's Den, which was less of a brothel and more of a home to them punters who'd be walking alone after spending all their money on fermented rhizomes. And whores galore, let us not forget; these were a class of men without regrets. Lest ye be judged in the house of the Lord – 'tis why we all neglect to attend our church, so that we may indulge in all of our favourite activities instead of beggin' on our knees to a figure we cannot see. We'd rather be drinkin' on a Sunday morning than spend the rest of our days on an idol with promises that cannot be kept. For years, we tried these unsuccessful attempts. We've cried, we've wept, but without reply, and even longer 'till the day we die. Now we're old men at age twenty-two, we'll most probably croak soon from drinkin' this brew. There's no need to be well behaved; let's say cheers to an early grave! And, on that day, we shall be locked away in a dark and dank dungeon, impossible to escape. In this state, we'll realize this weight and we'll soon forget that glorious fate. That's enough contemplation about these sorrows, let's now focus our thoughts on all the 'borrows'. 'Tis what we call our items of theft, for we were blessed by the Lord with God's gracious gift. To conceal and take, to earn a few bills, no time for faith; I choose free will.

Shanty II

♣

"Bottoms Up"

CRAWLING THROUGH SAND TO APPROACH THE CRASHING SEA, mankind applies the crudest method to sustain its energy. Mouth consumes the Ocean of secrets – soiled in salt, sand and debris; her punishment for his attempt to expose the vast sea. No regrets occur because, as often as it seems, pride always replaces man's well-being. The taste of dirty salt on the throat can exalt mankind of their incongruent nature. Like this floating bottle – scathed by the ebb and flow, shaped over decades, the bottle now eroded. Still quite weak and unknowing whether they be genuine, the stranger wades in the water to the alcohol collection. Scattered bottles of booze, clouded and stained, with no clue as to what they contained. Green glass filled with strange, brown liquid. Without hesitation, he downs the drifted in the hopes that he would soon be intoxicated and, consequentially, uplifted.

The message in the bottle is consumed and the contents are ignored, treating the seawater as one of his own whores.

Covered in bruises and with a foul, sweaty odour; stained with bodily fluids causing cracks in his leather. With a rather large belch, followed by a toothless grin, some mumbled words come spewing from within, out onto his chin – yet the words do not portray the thoughts of the gentleman inside. No words of worth enter nor penetrate the mind. Speaking in these conflicting manners, with the thoughts of a poet, yet like that of a scavenger. He emphasizes speech, for his ideals are unique; each character is a collection for his own boutique. A conflict is posed to the man of the external, while the other man inside writes it down in his journal. Two components working side by side, built on the conflict between well-being and pride. Funnily enough, he embraces it; the many masks he wears to conceal his wit.

And all the Ocean blue makes a man feel lost; an illusion is produced by confusion and lust. And so you down the poisonous brew, spilling her body through and through. You devour her salt, sand and debris, as she falls from the brim, carelessly spilling pebbles over the rim. The mask and the perpetuating lies are no longer debunked as he begins to feel the wrath of her body getting him drunk. As the cruelty of Nature absorbs more life, the cycle continues with each swallow of pride. The questions man once asked are eventually forgotten… and soon *his* nature becomes tastefully rotten.

♠ ♣ ♥ ♦

Real or imaginary, his eyes begin to see, there in the distance, one breached and one 'bout to sink. He watches the ship as she saves one last breath, as he watches the other moored in the depth. The Ocean floor's wracked by two man-made events: one of an anchor and another for the dead. The ship that was once claimed is now swirling down the drain – going down, deeper into lost rain. *So much sentiment in which past memories share so much meaning to me. A promise to myself on behalf of this breached brig: I will find it in my right to conquer that ship.*

Now it becomes clear how them bottles of beer floated to the shore and kept him from the fear. Secrets are the power of her. And, like the Ocean, the sinkin' ship spills some of her own hidden messages. Crates of cargo appear to be bottles of rum, gin and age-old brandy. So he gathers the flotsam for later use. With no company to share it with, he will forever choose. One by one, twelve crates be saved and dragged through the sand to a nearby cave. To hide away from men with superior pride, regardless of whom they are or what they may hide.

Unbeknownst to the stranger, an old man watches over. The line of his image was circling the stranger's periphery and, suddenly, the stranger became aware he was not alone.

You got nothing on me; I got everything you need.

The narcissism was displayed for all eyes to see. The old man had resided on the island for some time and could detect the slightest change in the seasonal tides. A man of vast knowledge full of wisdom of all kinds, yet the old man could not speak, as if his tongue were cut by the knife. You see, years ago he became marooned on his island. There were no other men to speak with for the years that followed. And, with no speech at all, his thoughts became enlightened; enriched by the beauty of that mysterious island. The old man suspected the stranger was in a terrible state, for he witnessed the man with a conflicting debate. He noticed how much pride the young stranger had portrayed, on top of these priorities 'twas the booze he most craved. The old man inferred a conflict that all men carry: a battle between his pride and well-being, the minority. So, the old man began to digress and thus no words would be said, and no ability to express.

The old man sought to help the poor stranger by draggin' his body over to his chambers. The old man was a mute and had no words to offer, yet was capable of communication by substituting speech with gesture.

I demand to stay on the beach to comb for crates. The old man didn't reply, just simply hesitated. *D'you think of me as a vagrant? By God, you must be ancient. Call me what you will. I've no patience for meaning; I choose the swill. To talk about philosophical revelations is a waste in its own right. These matters of God do not quench my appetite. I'll return to my cave, where I once hid my beauties away.*

But as the stranger desisted, he become rather faint. Desperately becoming rather much like a fool. Once again, he collapsed to the ground and drooled. Moving further away from this uninhabited land, he began to resist the old wise man.

7

The old man delivers his decrepit guest by providing sustenance and a bed to rest. Curiosity lures him to a closer view, but his sight was blinded by his craving for booze. And, moreover, the stranger mumbles in his sleep, while the old man notices the strangers crooked teeth. We may now call him 'Teefer' instead of 'stranger', since this name most suits his grotesque nature: causal pain can leave asymmetric cracks on the face, accumulated from a lifetime of harsh constraint. The old man glanced at his clothes, which smelled of cold smoke, all tattered and worn, with a Paris Beau hat that seemed to be torn. With many years spent on this land, the old man had time and patience to utilize his hands. Using fine bone and bristle for needle and thread, the worn hat had been restored in the shape of Teefer's head. While mending the hat, an eye glanced at the man in mid-sleep, and, just then, Teefer mumbled these words: *Black beach.*

Teefer's left eye began to pry open, noticing the old man no longer groping. Inspired by old thoughts in his mind, Teefer planned his escape, as done in his previous life. Suppressing his thirst left over from dehydration, instead kills the weakness by beating the iron. As stubborn as he was, he did this just because he enjoyed himself fully being his own boss. Remnants of vomit coated his raw throat, yet his only thoughts in this mode were of the black beach and the boat.

By reclaiming his might, he began to ignite; the little spark in his mind became a stick of dynamite. Uproar began between himself and the old man about his identity and his unknown position on this land.

Where am I from and who have I become?

These two questions are irrelevant to some, yet the confusion only reminded him of his craving for rum, and all his thoughts in his sleep were eventually forgotten.

Nevermore will I contain my pain. Nevermore as prisoner of yours. Rotate your neck and keep it closed; I scoff at the fool without wearing any clothes. You claim to be wise, but you're merely old and dirty. How can you match my level of worthy? Like a brute, you make yourself to be; you'll serve as my slave and you shall never trick me, nor will I allow you to speak freely on your own thoughts and beliefs. I'll have you locked and chained within that cave!

Teefer's anger dominated his wit. And, with no words spoken by the old man, he had no defence and thus no plan. As amnesia took its toll, habits became rather foul, and he became the man he wanted to be, in his eternal state of misery.

With no speech and no self-expression, the old man had provided no first impression. Yet the old man did not ignore the fact that he had a knife pointed at his back; he simply could not express to the man that they were both Gentlemen Jack. Old man agreed to obey the lad, should Teefer soon understand their personal pact. Nothing escapes this thriving mindscape: not the sea nor the sky. And, with no words to utter a verbal reply, thoughts perpetually flow through old man's mind:

May Teefer soon realize that the man he inherited has lived and died, then all will be demystified and therefore so will I.

Pushed and shoved by Teefer's driving rage, 'twas a symbol representing youth's violence on the aged. Old man was speechless, struck with terror and Whist. He was left to submit to the young man's fists. Out they both went through the foreign land to return to the view of blue seas and golden sand. They reached a height of Teefer's stance, as large as he was on top of this land. This perspective brought him to a higher ego, which was lying underneath his cracked face and Paris beau. *Thar she is – my glorious ship, breached on her side, having a kip!*

Smugly, with pride on the line, his eyes became blind. This man was almost lost inside his conflicted mind. He may never find himself in the core of his heart, since all his components had fallen apart. Then these men came pouring onto Teefer's island.

How dare they print their feet upon untouched sand! Outnumbered and exhausted, how will I conquer them? For it is I versus the world, and this crew of gentlemen. The only method of influence that I see fit is to manipulate them with guile, cunning and wit. With their minds all wet and calm from feeding them with my supply of rum, they will become absorbed in my charm and soon enough I will become their Captain.

And did them men soon arrive; men of all kinds: bandits, petty thieves and the like.

Come along, old man. These are our guests; let us have a laugh at their expense.

So down they both went, climbing down the familiar descent to meet and greet the lads and gents to prevent their consent. The old man knew the island well and had lived solo all his life. Still weeping, the old man waded through the trees and squatted behind a large boulder, with Teefer behind. With gun in hand and eyes on his prey, Teefer smiled at two Englishmen arguing on the bay.

They be British, thought the villain to himself. *Perhaps they be smugglers or bandits in search for wealth.*

With one eye fixated on this savage band, the other eye tells the story of a boy becoming a man. His green face reveals the whole story as his mind becomes conflicted. His youth was being ignored by these superficial misfits.

I think you'll find this land is mine, and don't think twice about wasting my time. All these rows and arguments never end when you're dealing with the dignity of grotesque men.

Lads, gentlemen, we cannot fight for there are greater fortunes if our minds combine. Allow me to introduce myself, my name is Prize, said the ego in disguise from that previous life. *I be the first mate; our captain had died, 'twas his unfortunate fate. I told him what for, he simply ignored. He did not listen. Now he has departed, and we do not miss him.*

Uniting with these men, Teefer began drinking and learnt the men were ex-sailors, now prisoners of the King. Since no bugger held them down, they were free to roam. They be fugitives of a land without a crown and throne. So Teefer conjured up a plan to manipulate.

I will get them all drunk with me bottles and crates. The men will cheer for me assuming me Captain. And as he ponders his scheme, the book changes its chapter.

Shanty III

♥

Inebriated

WITH YOUNG, BOYISH LOOKS, DARK EYES AND SHORT HAIR, with dimples on each cheek, me appearance is quite fair. Rather lanky and thin, I escaped me shackles on a whim. Albeit not manly, we'll give you that, but what we lack we make up for in competing with the lads. Rather generous to the common folk, we pay for rounds of alcohol, so no one will sulk. Not around this fellow; no lad around us is mellow, despite the victims of theft and the miserable weather. Gained quite the reputation, me. Claimin' many titles here. They mostly know us as 'Jack the Lad', who'd most endeared. 'Gentleman Jack' was me preferred; 'tis what me bird, Ms Lyon, referred. We's also heard the name 'Jack the scallywag'; them jealous punters called me this, especially when we be utterly pissed. Jack Trade was me carpenter's name, for we're no master at the game; still, we try. Me birth name is John after me brother who died young, but we resent this name, though reason we have none.

♠ ♣ ♥ ♦

Becoming confident with alcohol, but weak without, you continue to drink rum, ale and thick, black stout. Drink up, lads; man knows best. Black and tan will grow hairs on your chest. Avoiding the back mirror, as you resent your own face. Slamming doors behind, like you own the damn place. Man must learn to walk away from the crumbling of his past and drink the last of what's in the bottom of the cask. Share the spoils; let's have another pint. We fancy a bit o' wheat ale, light; we've that kind of appetite. So close the curtain and prevent that sight; shut all the doors to block the sunlight. This memory shall not be remembered. Wishful thinking is mostly entertained from the bouts of heavy drinking 'till memories become stained. Drag us from this place, from this time, from ourselves. All for the sake of our own damn health.

Yesterday, we'd been drinkin' French champagne. Nowadays, we'd be kippin' beneath the window pane. Today, we'd be drinking just like the rich. Tonight, we'll be sleepin' under the tower bridge. Why? For we're drunk and skint. Nothing in our pockets, 'tis but dust and lint. The bitterness of pride and ale always requires acquirement. We've acquired a taste for what tastes bitter. But ale is much sweeter nowadays, especially with that tobacco haze. Inhale thick smoke and feel ease from that flame;

feel better for short moments, exchanging poison for a day. Drink up for the second, the ale's ready for the taking. Embrace your pride and forget the shaming. You ask me why we drink? We's never been wrong. And, as long as we are right, we will continue to beat the iron. We down more alcohol to drown any remaining regret to remove ourselves from the guilt that we've been building in our heads.

As the ale takes hold of us, the shapes of the world become a circus. The shapes remain static 'till we glance to clarify, which gets us dancing with the motion in reply. Perplexed by the complex, but, conceptually, we know that we are the object of the movement. As our eyeballs play tricks we laugh hysterically in encouragement. We drink a bit more ale and continue to chuckle like politicians. We sense the people around us feeling very smooth in submission. Oh, the flesh of any ol' tramp would suffice to reach an ecstatic level of surprise.

Walking in a random direction we never know or seem to pay attention to or care about our whereabouts, and now we fall straight on our faces, but never the ale we blame. And then there's me, spewing out all the history, so that we may continue drinking throughout the evening, but in secret we'll be feelin' that misery. Every night, as we stroll alone, we face the cobblestones on our way home, while our own identity is unknown.

The obsessive depression dictates our vision's tension. Thoughts unknown to no other, leaves us hanging in bother. Gazing on that page where concrete is laid, vomiting where the stone is paved. To us, it seems rather trite, despite the fact that it is broad daylight. Startled by lost desire and draining in the mire, like the stains of booze in Covent's gravel; tearin' in the eyes as each drop fell. We never waste our time with any synthetic particulars. Only, the glory spills through our fingers like pieces of sand falling through our hands; no strength to grip them, no thoughts to understand. We walk helplessly here in our discourse, no methods to divorce our pain and remorse.

Shanty IV

♦

"All Hands on Deck"

THAT NIGHT ON THE ISLAND WAS PARTICULARLY COLD; ALL surrounded the yellow fire, 'cept a childe and the old. They kept quiet in the shadows over yonder, while the men exchanged stories of whoring squanders. Prize began sharing his line of women, from his sweetest of treats to dirty old hags. The men all listened to his sexist remarks; 'twas if it were his own stag. To some degree, you might agree with me, but what drew the attention was Prize's cheeky reputation. But, actually, everything was not as it appeared to be, as this was all part of Trade's fantasy.

All men 'cept the old had laughed at Prize's stories, for he was a rather charismatic one and not at all boring. He entertained the men with his sleight of hand, besting gestures all round including the old man's. But what the crew were oblivious to was the fact that Prize was not telling the truth. Prize's main flaw, other than enduring whores, was his obsession with being superior, hence making him a shifty liar. Yet the only man who knew of his black heart was the old man, who caught him cheating in cards.

This evidence was witnessed during the exchange of business among men of trickery, to prove themselves courageously. The game of choice was well known to the boys: a game called All Fours; a card game for two or more. Players win by making tricks from thin air to obtain the highest score. The old man noticed that, when Prize received his hand, he'd exchange his new cards for ones buried in the sand. Yet old man was not in the position to accuse the young man, for he himself had no speech and no respect from this savage clan. So he kept this in mind, continuing to watch over the players, evaluating the men in this game of betrayal.

All men told stories of how they spent their life: robbin' earls and peasants, getting caught, and serving time. Many had claimed they were merely innocent, which of course was another lie. One man by the name of Guido had admitted his crime of treason. He attempted to destroy parliament for all the wrong reasons. That, being his attempt for anarchy, was all for the greater cause: to come down hard on the elite, ending established law. He told us all that he gathered his crew of rebels to plan his plot, but just as he was about to light the fuse, the authorities had him caught. Now he is here on this hellish land, without a method for revenge. He was brought here by our glorious King without a trial, thus no defence.

Then there was the twin of Guido – that be Mr Gulliver; you could not tell the boys apart for they be identical brothers. But there were some features that were diverse that be the expression on their distinct faces. While Guido had a destructive taste, Mr Gulliver preferred creations. Take one look at Guido and you'll see he's quite irate; perhaps developed from his pyromania, he developed a sense of hate. Take another look and you may infer that the twin you see is Mr Gulliver. His creative behaviour may elude potential danger, for he served many years as the ship's doctor. A practical man with skilful hands, more so than the old man, who'd spent years on this land. From surgeon to carpenter, sharing talents with the Knave, Mr Gulliver was a man whom Teefer'd most craved.

This man will come in handy, thought Teefer while drinking brandy.

Of these drunken, dodgy men, one man was the least sober; he had no time to think for himself, for the man was always hungover. Because he was a drunken ol' bastard, all had call him 'Sod'. This particular epithet most suited this greasy fellow, for he too suffered from an intrinsic fraud. He did have some talent, mind you, being a chef as well as singing a tune or two. And, coincidentally, he'd whistle in his speech, which was caused by the gap between his two front teeth.

He'd sing some songs as like a glorious angel, before blurting out nonsense to the commune. He held major responsibilities, because he was always drinking so carelessly. Nevertheless, the crew required such a bastard as they had grown to love him so dearly. Like the village idiot who sits, laughs and falls off the wall, he became the local comic (not completely useless after all). He'd be in charge of cheering the men, when they be saddened by the seashore. He'd drink with any who needed a drink; you really couldn't ask for more.

Sitting behind the drunken, ol' Sod was a miserable man – a recluse at a loss. 'No man is an island' was the motto he'd mumble to himself. He'd refused to acknowledge the detriment to his health. Yet no solution would remove the burden of his lifelong guilt. It accumulated more weight on his shoulders, which he had forever built. This wretched man named Solomon Blay had sat all alone, away from the game of cards and fire – planted solo on his naked throne.

No man cares to sympathize with another man's shame; 'tis why I choose to analyse my deep and profound pain. As if legend had lived and died, and ended with his dying name, thought Blay to himself as ashes collect from the flames.

Old nightmares will motivate this character into solitude, while other men contribute to the social mood. All men nullify this absurdity by justifying the perversity. Blay would be on the crow's nest as the chief rigger, since he detested the others for being inconsiderate. With that, all was settled: Solomon Blay would have his own part of the vessel. To agree with them, he had nothing to say, so Guido picked up a log, which in the fire he placed. While the fire began to stoke, out came Prize to break the ice with another uncouth joke. Soon the men learnt to forget Blay's demeanour and woes; he laid back silently in the background of the black, unseen in the shadows.

The next hand won was by the cheeky, tricky boy, Mr Prize, for he'd got 'all the fours', thus fooling everyone's eyes. Calm as a coma, sharp as a dart, proud as a pistol, right from the start. A card sharp; he's got Aces up his sleeve – that'd be what Prize would have everyone believe. *All those people seem so feeble. Why don't they leave? Why do they stay? Begging on their knees like weasels before me. They will surely believe anything I tell, anything I say.*

Prize's grin had become rather wide, such that all treats and hags on the side would be terrified to see his gold teeth shimmering in the darkness, sheathing the true nature of his starkness. Yet the old man knew, as he continued to watch, the young lad was cheating while drinking Teefer's scotch. And did them men cheer like dirty men with beer, especially William Blyth, who'd set the atmosphere. You see, William Blyth, also known as 'Bill the Knife', would show teeth to your face while he be sleeping with your wife. There'd be a counterattack from a Knife in the back if you're not careful of Bill Blyth's wrath. He had a grin to die for, but you could never trust him, for he was helping himself to more of Teefer's gin.

But the man to fear most was Sir Edward Thatcher; this Goliath-like man had the strength of ten bastards. Black-bearded and smoke steamin' from his head, he were a man with no quarrels for his biceps were lead. He was the ships loader, haulin' barrels in the hold, for he had more strength than the men in control. With his strength, Thatcher could kill all at the top of this guild, knocking down the castle that Teefer had built. Teefer manipulated Thatcher by exploiting his weakness: the sort of pride that deals with fitness. Yet no names were given to a man of this kind, for his name 'Thatcher' was already dignified. All trod lightly when his mind was speakin', for no other soul would dream of being beaten by a man who weighed down the world with one foot. Perhaps now you understand the significance of this book: all these men were part of Jack's ego – caricatures of pride to hide away the greatest lie.

And, finally, we turn to the narrator: a lady disguised as a gent. The omnipotent soul of all that is whole in this fable of destruction and descent. Edif O'Neal be the neutral party; without a flaw of emotion, she be explainin' all this commotion to the mysterious man who'd thrown it all away and who maintains his mask to conceal his face.

Inside the pandemics, the mindscape of man, I relate all these horrors to the rest of the band.

Shanty V

♠

Nemesis

WE BEGAN THIS WORK IN SOLO, YET ONCE CAUGHT IN THE market of Soho. You see, in this part o' town, all the loot and stolen goods pass though Jonathan Wilde and all his crew of goons. Every now and then, Wilde pretends he's one of us. Occasionally, we'll witness a smile or a cheeky sneer of lust. Since he bribed that copper, we be tethered to his pockets. Like that of a child, for John Wilde there be no mutual respect from that thief-taker. Despite all this, we take our own pleasure, fencing goods to him for that personal treasure.

Then came the punters who failed to reciprocate, like rats scrounging around, searchin' for a method to escape. They'd be leaning on my earnings, as if mine were theirs. My borrows be earned honestly, yet they be splitting hairs. They'd say:

*Look lively, you're driving us mad. You'd had plenty
of chances by spending and lending advances. Lay down,
lay low. Pay me your earnings; pay what you owe. We're
on every corner, so you can't ignore my woe. Just you wait
and see; you wait until the end. You give me some of that
horrible money, and we'll be your closest friend.*

Around we went with this redundant argument, so we
called him a cunt and had done with it. Watch and learn,
as he takes the piss by taking a risk. Watch and learn, as we
forsake our right to be free. Watch and learn, as we break
our knees spilling our guts with each of these, only to then
protect a master thief. Only one name rings a bell: that be
Jonathan Wilde, may he rot in Hell. He's a sheep dressed
in wolves' clothing – self-loathing, boasting and gloating.
Smug about the position, but in secret he'd be wishin' that
he'd be the King of the blessed and the sinned, of the light
and the dark, of the bride and the groom, and everybody
else in the sodding room. One by one, we'd like to smack
'em right and show 'em our might, 'till the bleeders fight.
But not with our fists, that be the hero's way. We'd use a
heavy, blunt object for our message to convey. This cold
heart, with all its sins, shows no compassion when the rain
comes pouring in.

Brutal is mutual when you get that nonsense again
from another equal and a sequel will always continue to
revolve around me and you. We'll flick the knocker on his
door; knock chips off that wood, and knock his bleedin'
teeth out, as we bloody well should. We've no bother for
these dangers; we'll die without fear. It'll be in one ear and
out the other; do I make myself clear? We've no bother for

his whimper; we'd prefer it much simpler. So, we worked it out with our own simple methods. 'Tis but restless and reckless of the pride, of the shame, the glory in the game, and everything is mine for the taking.

But then, and only then, we were framed once again and touched by the cold. 'Twas a sting, left us in the dead winter without a moment to sink in, and so Wilde's manipulation begins. 'Tis the final sin. We felt betrayed – strangled with a blade. Tie a rope around our necks and squeeze 'till we behave.

We thought it was a joke; 'twas too easy to ignore the mess, but then it slowly crept into our thought process. We stand in formation, not dare to hesitate. Focusing on the back of his neck, with eyes straight. But, wait, this can't be our fate. This abusive banter among Wilde's crew was aimed to be obtrusive, so we must obey the privileged few. But shouldn't our gentleman's mission be without this juxtaposition? We witnessed in the entrance way at least a dozen crew members at bay. Forever driven by words of dismay and perhaps wisdom, but we do not follow this tradition. No thoughts override the pride of the heathen, whatever the reason.

So our nightmare became his dream. Exploring his loathing, he discovers a new trophy. A flavour to boast with, in light of them all joking. Revolving around that revolting sound, and throwing his weight around the town. That be Mr Wilde, with his gang of thieving clowns. All them punters crowd around to taste the available. Sucking on the wheat and wood, those sycophants are so gullible, as they bloody well should. They want a taste of the ether world; may they be worthy. Most of the soppy buggers have no taste buds left, but they are always thirsty.

They're not concerned about the world they choose when the system is rigged and you're born to lose. 'Tis no concerns of mine; we'll gladly drink more booze and wine. *Take a swig of that, Jack,* says our partner in crime. So we down the liquid and it drifts down the spine. Sing it loud and make one proud. Sing it out, that revolting sound. The only thing that bothers are these men who call me their brothers, their arms in need. They be greedy; no different from me. Still, we won't refrain. We can't complain. We shan't ascertain whether they be too simple for the brain. As a matter of fact, we quite like that, to abuse our colleagues and the rest of the pack. We're better off stealing from these poor little blighters paying their taxes blindly without learning the facts. The fact is that we are all raiders and we see the denials with our own two eyes. We witnessed the victims in broad daylight. We felt compelled to expel ourselves from all those traits long ignored. So treat them like savage strangers escorting their whores.

SHANTY VI

♣

"WITH FLYING COLOURS"

THE ADVENTURE WAS TIMELESS, WITH ITS ENDLESS SEAFRONT horizon shimmering in the moonlight like stacked, crumpled, animated pages; like those of Brighton. The texture of the sky was creamy and the colour was maroon blending into a smoked black. Around the blazing fire, each man matched the stack and took his play, continuing to best each other within this man's game. With cards in hand, a drunken Sod poses a backhander, exposing his hand to the other bystanders. Those who were lucky were inconsiderably loathed by the men of grotesque nature, all tattered by the clothes. Losing at the man's table they may curse, but never cry. Man must never express his tears; he must maintain this lie. The weakness is suppressed to elude these immature feelings, replaced them all with anger, to dominate the weaklings. You may prefer your anger to hide, displaying your pride, than be bawlin' and crestfallen 'till you commit suicide.

Men continued to exchange stories 'bout whores, borrows and ink. Braggin' 'bout their 'trophies on arms', with no capacity left to think. Most, if not all, had an anchor drawn on their upper-right arm; 'twas a symbol of their charm. Traits such as these were of the lowest class, especially without a gov'nor proudly wearing their brass. Yet the old man had none of the above, hence the lack of wit and charm. 'Twas no method to compete with the grotesque of the young. So, he continued to sulk in silence, without a word to utter, while the young cabin childe had been sobbin', developin' a stutter. The childe was afraid of all these men, for he had been cornered time and time again. Just as the lads had told him: *Men don't cry!* His feelings were suppressed by the gents who were themselves unqualified. The fatherless childe was kept this way by the abuse and neglected innocence. And now the young childe was another example – a victim of cognitive dissonance. In silence, the childe did not say a word; yet, in violence, children should be beaten and not heard.

And just then did Teefer remember that dream he'd had while still under. 'Twas a state that felt familiar, as all dreams feel when they begin to disappear. *The features of the dream were of a Black beach*, said Teefer, beginning his persuasive speech. *I tell you, lads and gents alike, the dream was so clear to me. We must rebuild this ship to find the mysterious Black Beach. I've envisioned an island hiding Nature's rarest treats, from precious stones to hidden secrets and many other delicacies. We'll take what's ours, leaving*

*no remains behind. Come with me, my fellow men, let's see
what we can find.*

So the crew agreed to come along, such that they could
drink Teefer's rum. And then the game of manipulation
had truly begun.

"Then, to see how like a King I dined too, all alone and
attended by my servants. Prize, as if he had been my favourite,
possessed a gift of the utmost fervour; the old man, who had
now grown very old and crazy, sat always at my right hand;
the twin brothers, Guido on one side of the table and Gulliver
on the other, complimented me by opposing each other; and
the rest of the rats expected, every now and then, a bit from
my hand, as a mark of special favour."[1]

A few drinks here and a few laughs there, and all
become old friends. Yet the fate of these mates was difficult
to tell and impossible to comprehend. For the dream was a
ruse – a method to excuse the stranger from being judged
by the old man's views – and then the dream was being
used to motivate and amuse; to manipulate these pawns
'twas Teefer's method of abuse. Uniting these villains
began to accumulate the foundation of all men's hate. The
hate of mankind versus the pride of themselves was all at
the expense of their own damn health.

All louts laze about from ale, hours before, no doubt.
All except childe, who'd hide in his Cribbage, warily
waiting for the boisterous British.

♠ ♣ ♥ ♦

1.   Adopted from *Robinson Crusoe* by Daniel Defoe.

The following day came; first woke Teefer with a headache and a body all sore from the night before. His hair and clothes smelled of fire wood, which reminded him of his early childhood. With plain eyes, he recognized that he be in the company of these parasites. He'd wake them up the old-fashioned way, with a cold splash of water slashed straight to the face. One by one, he awoke them all, 'cept Edward Thatcher, who'd drunk more alcohol. He was a big lad (who could handle that), but when he was havin' a nap no bugger dared wake the lad. He was left there peacefully alone, all because his biceps were as hard as stone.

All of them viewed the plan to restore the ship, drawn the previous night by Mr Gulliver, the chief carpenter and the newly recruited shipwright. *A few repairs to the hull and she'll be as right as rain. When the tide is high, we may careen to work on the bottom frame. Though with a hole in her belly, she's not completely destroyed; we shall name her 'Providence', after the deliverance of mankind.*

Immediately, the men obeyed, despite their frivolous pride. Teefer knew how to command them all by looking them stern in the eyes. As one does with one's dog, which obeys every word; with a sharp gaze, master dominates – 'tis the method of the bastard.

Gulliver returned to the ship to retrieve all tools from the hull. And just then did Thatcher awake, despite the ache in his skull. His motives were driven solely by the necessity to demonstrate his strength, almost excessively. While most men sawed wood in pairs, Thatcher had pulled trees out with his bare hands. Then there was Sod, who'd begun drinkin' the previous night and continued on to the next mornin', in broad daylight. He'd been doin' his best in his own mode, by entertainin' the lads and takin' the piss out of Guido. Naturally, Guido repelled his brother's advice; he started his own project, creating dynamite. Acquired from recent Trade voyages from Indonesia, stowed away in the ship were volcanic sand deposits smelted from cinnabar. The next ingredient was saltpetre, acquired from nearby caves. The substance was a mix of bat droppings and moisture from the crashing waves. He scraped the secrets of her, fragments of the stalagmites, filtered by the sea to quench his appetite. The last ingredient would be charcoal, collected from campfire debris. With a stone and rock, he milled the lot and placed the powder within his sock. When Sod saw this, he could not resist; he took the piss, informing all what they had missed. No laughter came from Blay who was closed indefinitely; he longed too much for the loneliness of the sea. Neither old man nor childe were with the right company to express themselves freely without penalty. They kept quiet, cutting down trees, while Teefer, Prize and Bill the Knife agreed to discuss their scheme.

♠ ♣ ♥ ♦

Three days of route and the ship was absolute. Old planks and tree root were used for scraps of firewood. Timber was gathered and cut into planks, replacing new with old, equivalent to their ranks. Yet a flag they did not have, which would fly over their heads. The men had no King nor country; they were practically dead. Devouring the secrets of that peaceful sea. Without a care in the world, which was always to be. To the death, one will discover one's prospects, promises since one's birth. Developed into the complex, for better or for worse, that – for all mankind – each feels more entitled than the others, while ignoring that innate dependence once received from their mothers.

The day had come to set sail on the seas; all the men had their functional duties, gathering necessities. Gluts and gluts of coconuts were amassed by shaking trees, to fulfill Thatcher's empty guts and the rest of the SOBs.[2] A craftsman of rarity, Gulliver had made a seine by spending time twisting vine and utilizing his brain. He stole from the Ocean blue, like a common thief, taking colourful fish from the shallow waters of the reef. Even Sod had helped by writing a couple o' shanties, but he could not express true words of the soul without a drop o' the good ol' brandy. So quite naturally, he indulged himself in Teefer's spirits to allow his tongue to became more fluid, after all he was British. Guido can be described as having an unusual design; he was the most inclined to destroy all mankind. His main tasks were to burn the stakes gathered by childe and old man. The larger the fire, the greater fortune for the journey to the black sand. His instructions were well understood, so he burnt the remaining scrap wood. After he had finished his task, he continued to render his fine, black substance. But, soon after quenching the fire, suspicions leered to his absence.

Prize and Bill the Knife assigned duties to the lower-ranking mates. As men followed their orders, their

2.   Silly old bastards.

31

egos did inflate. Teefer assumed the role of the crew's new Captain, while Prize and Bill planned their move to overtake the manipulation. The pride of Prize was smothered in lies, as he resented the ascent of the benign. In his spare time, he designed a method to quench his nefarious appetite. Bill embodied the anthropomorphic personification of jealousy, within this mindscape of one committing an unscrupulous felony. And so, like a game of draughts or chess, each took their turn trying their best to dominate the rest. But now in the centre was Mr Teefer, who'd established a crew of little, rotten bleeders. 'Twas an abstract maze of psychological burden, exploiting pride and turning their weaknesses against them. By pressing the bruise of the lost and confused, Teefer was using the men for his amusement, and, with this method, he was destined to be the prime abuser.

SHANTY VII

♥

PURLOIN AND TIME

IN THE BEGINNING, WAS TREVOR DOYLE; HE WAS A RIGHT CARD. We called him 'Clever Trevor', as he sang like a bard. He could sing a tune or two before blurtin' out his digested brew. So, he was a main character in our lively crew. You could ask 'im anything; no problem was too big for his sort. Only a few times was he unlucky and the coppers had him caught. He was the fella that taught us our tricks. I've known 'im for years, since we were ten and six. Over the years, he taught us a thing or two about the art of pickpocketing. The ol' bump and take was his method of abuse. One trick that all we Londoners use.

It's a simple strategy to feed yourself. No tools required, but agility and stealth. Simply mind your own and then bump into a stranger. With a swift rummage to ransack through the course of rearrangement. Pickpocketing 'em

is without a doubt the best, for they don't suspect a single
thing swiped from the vest. It's the simplest way to leave
no trace, but if you're not too careful, it may put you in
your place and the next thing you know is you're being
chased. If you're caught, they chuck you in Newgate. That's
what happened to us once or twice. We were caught red-
'anded and had to pay the price. But we don't regret it,
quite the contrary; this is the sanctuary where we learnt
all the tricks of the trade. 'Tis where we met all our mates.

Do as you please, to your hearts content. Swipe a few
bits and pieces, and sell it to your fence, so that later you
can buy a round for the gents. It's an art to keep up the
thrill, and the action has been fantastic. The ol' bump
and take is the oldest trick in the book, which makes it a
classic. But, just so you know, I'll tell you something real.
It ain't too bad of a deal. It's a bargain; it's a steal.

Then you got Joseph 'Blueskin' Blake, once employed
by Jonathan Wilde. Melancholy as he was, the man had
never smiled. Blueskin hated Wilde, for sending him to
the hangman, yet Blueskin escaped his sentence and later
joined our clan. There be me, Jack Trade, the jail breaker,
and me arch nemesis Wilde the thief-taker, fence and
traitor. Wilde had influence on both sides of the law;
both thieves and coppers served as his whores. Wilde was
treasonous to our community; to him, we were pawns of
opportunity. So, when Wilde asks us to fence our goods to
him, we reply by gobbing on his shin. A thick lob of spit
comes deep from within and flies across the way, sending
a message that 'we will not obey'. And because of that
action, we began our own faction.

Price tags were patronizing, descending us into poverty. Allocated to the private classes of the richest noblemen and monarchy. So you take a little bit more to pay for entertainment forms: booze and whores.

Once caught – grassed up by me brother – they send you to court to defend your honour. Before that moment came, they chucked me in the holding cell, givin' me a taste of England's version of Hell. We hadn't reached our prime, and we've all served some time, but not for too long. A spade smuggled in and soon we'll be gone. A razor or a file to pick at the shackles; we break out of prison and we're soon in cackles. Dig a hole in the roof, smash through the tiles and soon we'll be back at the Den laughin' in style. Hitch a ride from a wagon, and we'll be with Ms Lyon, braggin'.

Not last week but the week before, four-and-twenty sinners came knocking on our door. As we ran out the back, they ran in. They beat us down with their rolling pins. We may have committed the crime, but we're never guilty. Not when the victims are sinners; all dirty and filthy. No one is pure; we are all raw to the core. We all possess features of thieves, so Mr Judge, Your Honour, we plead 'not guilty'. He sent us to Newgate Prison for this petty behaviour, but one hour later we were back in our chambers. That be due to Ms Elizabeth Lyon, with a file and a disguise. We'd be walking out the gates dressed like the wives of some ol' dandy, which became rather handy. And one hour later we'd be back at the Den, sippin' at the ol' brandy.

The tools we used were from the early craft of

carpentry; plus, these days we'd acquired the skill of locksmithery. The prison locks are simple to manipulate: a simple nail will do between the latch and face plate. Apply a bit of pressure and a wiggle to the latch, and soon you'll find the catch and, with a sharp scratch, the lock should detach. Some locks are impossible to pick, so smash the fucker off; that should do the trick. Once the shackles have been removed, next you'll need to break through the roof. Use the nail that you found on the ground and like chisel and mallet, scrape a crack in the palette. Work on the crack 'till a hole appears, then hoist yourself up when the coast is clear. Finally, you've reached the roof of the prison; now it's time to lower yourself, so listen. Make a rope from the bed linen and tie it around a metal bar, but, when climbing down, it may be too far, so you're better off jumping onto a platform of some kind and before you realize you're back at the Den, serving time drinkin' fine wine.

The problem lies with being wanted and tipsy – a misfortune predicted by the local gypsy:

You keep doin' what you do, and they'll have your head, but we never listened to what she predicted. So off we went again, back in the slammers. Large iron doors bang in unison like a thousand hammers. But out we go again, as we find another method to escape Newgate Prison before being sentenced to our beheading. And there we all stand, one to the left another to the right. Thieves with nooses, side by side; cheating the hangman one last time.

Shanty VIII

◆

"Dead in the Water"

A T SEA, ALL CREW MEMBERS WERE ASSIGNED TO FUNCTIONAL positions, despite the fact that some lacked the ambition. Gulliver was responsible for the health of the men and ship. He had the most advanced skills of all, as he was the least unfit. But his part of the story had not yet emerged, so he waited for his turn by the stern. Alongside Master Gunner Guido, Edward Thatcher was deep in the hull, loadin' cannons and preparing for trouble. Thatcher was purposely delegated to do all the heavy liftin', to make him proud of his irrelevant strength and to prevent him from thinking. Solomon Blay was left doing things his own way up in the crow's nest. Frustration was sensed in the hesitation of his breath, so he was placed there all alone to deal with his painful distress. None of the lads were capable of sharing his remorse or listening to his story to identify the source of his own damnation, be it guilt or be it shame. He was his own worst enemy and had only himself to blame. Sod was chosen to be our chef to cook some lovely food, while gentlemen of the very best planned the next move. And, by concealing my identity, I was also assigned work. Adding daily entries into the Captain's log, I became the ship's clerk. Yet, in my spare time, I remain in my berth, writing it down in my journal, reporting to you about this crew in this damned state of the eternal.

From the lowest to the highest ranks, all men were on duty; Teefer as the Captain and old man as a swabbie. Seemingly, the old man had been assigned to unjust labour, while all the other convicts were being praised for their behaviour. Yet most were unaware that the swabbie was rather vital, 'twas a method for conditioning the wood for seaman's survival. So the old man proudly took the position and continued to swab all floors; like King Sisyphus to the god of war, he obeyed submissively in spite of it all. So you see, the old man was flawed after all, just like the rest of the mugs onboard.

Blay had been alone and with no glimmer of hope; the weight he had carried meant he could no longer cope. He tossed himself right off the boat, while the men all laughed as if it were a joke. But, when the men finally searched for poor ol' Blay, the conclusion was reached that he'd drowned that day. There was no sign of his body; perhaps he was lost at sea or perhaps the weight of his shame made his body sink. Yet, as his body could not be seen, he must not be dead; thus no grievin' be needed. Blay was sullen, sulking quietly in the riggin', and, like all the others, his true identity was hidden. But what was he thinking? Was he thinking at all? Was he pondering the end of days, fantasising about his fall, like the martyr who sacrifices his own quintessence? Providing an end to all the elements of man's obsolescence.

In these times, I can no longer lie; myself I despise. This shame, I admit, has made me commit the horrendous act of suicide. I cannot express my soul in regret; 'tis my own flaw of sinning. Don't you know I've always been feeling me best? I confess to you as my face be grinnin'. You acknowledge my worthy, as my teeth be all wordy; I appear so grotesque, me gums bleedin' from scurvy. And me hair be all curly from one of its symptoms. 'Tis why I seem shy, as I'm a simple victim of your God; you see, he has abandoned me – sending me to Hell with this awful disease. And now I've been quarantined, kept to myself, all for the sake of your own damn health. So, to acquit you all from this burden, I have ended my life without putting a word in.

Faithlessly yours,
Solomon Blay, Master Rigger

Isolated from the world and escaped in desperation; Blay was a coward filled with hesitation. There's no need for this sad act, for these men are on a mission; they need (not want) to discover their position. That is to say, the message they convey is to unleash their mistakes to seek ultimate freedom.

♠ ♣ ♥ ♦

Below the upper deck, within the brig's galley, Sod had been nurturing his own hidden fallacy. Built on the greed that all mankind carries, brewing up a concoction for the jolly and the merry. Acquiring a loaf of stale, ol' bread developing a grey and turquoise mold, he submerged the brick within his batch of mature, cold ale from the hold. The loaf had consumed all flavours of the brew; saturated and stewed, all remnants were imbued. *A masterpiece made from the finest ingredients: a dish fit for a King. And, to top it all off, a dash of rum, brandy, whisky and gin. Get that down ya gullet!* said the chef to himself with a jolly, ol' smile, as he downed the lot, the contents of the pot, to boost the crew's morale.

Underneath the feet of the Sod were two within the arsenal; they be Mr Guido and another complete asshole. Thatcher grunted as he lifted heavy weights proudly in his gymnasium, while Guido was using these lower decks for working on his latest. Like a mad genius with reassuring soliloquy, Guido's discourse was caustic and toned with villainy. He discussed with himself his plans of social anarchy, by planning to abolish the regime established by the monarchy. He fiddled with natural chemicals and substances of all kinds, following alchemical recipes to build a strange device – which would dice your limbs and blow your head to bits, shredding you to a million pieces!

Destructive thoughts struck a match in his mind; retribution was the reason, not spite nor treason. You see, long ago, Mr Guido was a Roman Catholic believer, overwhelmed by the Protestant reformation, for which he was not too eager. During the reign of King James I, common appraisal had become dispersed, to which the King outlawed his faith, hence Guido's vengeful taste. And yet, in the midst of his scheme, word got around to the King, who sent guards to the scene. Manifested by a dream, to assassinate the King was his argument. Yet the guards soon found his barrels of gunpowder beneath the Houses of Parliament. Tortured in the Towers, Guido submitted all his powers, naming all involved in the Gunpowder Plot. Yet, before he entered Hell, he had escaped from his cell, and – with the aid of his silent followers – he'd fled in his yacht.

The Ocean of Peace is truly my sanctuary. My escape from captivity. They'll never find me.

Thatcher, on the other hand, had a different story – one that was well told among the lads in all their glory. You see, as a young boy, residing in the port of Bristol, Thatcher had eye-witnessed the return and dismissal of many sailors, exchanging exotic goods and myth. As Thatcher had aged, he had marked his grave by enlisting in the Royal Navy, through which he gained his way to a seafaring escape. When Queen Anne's War had ended, he had descended into a life of piracy in order to pay for his unjust greed.

Sharing quarters beneath the hull would often lead to collision. You see, unlike Thatcher, who was filled with rage, Guido had a purpose and a vision. 'Tis why Guido admired Teefer, for he, too, had a goal in mind. The curiosity about Teefer's plans had soothed his appetite. So, quite naturally, Guido resented the boisterous hostility residing in these lower decks. He'd much prefer Teefer as his Narcissus to the Machismo complex. But, in the heat of a debate with Goliath the Irate, the voice of a childe cried out to the syndicate:

Sir! Sir! Please come quick! I think the chef has had too much to drink. Sir, I beg you. Please come quicker, he's bathed every vein in his body with liquor. He's lying on the ground with his head in vomitus. He's not comin' round; come, follow us.

Both men shuffled in urgency; they did not dilly-dally. They violently shoved the childe aside, finding Sod in the galley. His body was cold; his skin had turned blue.

Looks like he be poisoned from drinkin' his own brew.

At this point, all the men had witnessed what had happened. They laughed away at this fool's mistake for drinkin' without an end.

Too much of the poison, by the looks of it, said the Knife, resembling Teefer's grin. *He's repulsive, look at 'im. He's repulsive. He couldn't even handle his gin. And yet he was such a terrific lad for always makin' me laugh. So let's all say a few words and have a drink on his behalf.*

A few words more, and the men all poured themselves a tankard of ale. A few laughs here and a few tears there, cried in cheer for the cold and stale. Ale downed and tankards dropped, as was Sod, who'd been hoisted and tossed. The stale ale went down smoothly, as did Sod's cold body. There was no respect and no care for the sea because this friend was dear to the team. A stale, ol' rotter will find its way to the bottom, and no fish would eat this ol' mug or any other thug.

Shanty ix

♠

God's Gracious Gift

WE LEAVE THE PUB AND, ON THE WAY HOME, WE PASS BY THE church to see that Holy glow. But our feet keep walking as the guilt keeps stalking. We walk alone after pissin' and moanin' the night away. When the ale begins to flow, we ignore those boring shapes. Swallowing each foot print, knocking on the small world. We find something more to drink, shortly after we hurl. And, just like that, the nausea made our colours inverse; it couldn't possibly get any worse. A man's hand prays and speaks to God, not asking for any favours; we just spit it out from our gobs. All slurry like a bit o' drunken banter. Perhaps it'll take Him years to recognize our slander.

He doesn't want to know, and there's nothing that we owe: not one penny – not too few and not too many. If He don't ask for penance, we won't ask for love. We've made our peace with this brown ale, so we forget the man from up above who had us failed. It isn't even worth the argument to question the meaning. Is it worth it to control these feelings? Or is it worth listening to every ego who rejects God to host his own show? Play the game; it's always been this way. Nothing ever changes; it's always the same.

It's not truly our purpose, but what's worse is that we knew and accepted, and put our life on this bet that we would end up like this. A life without God – is it nonsense or bliss? Shall we allow this to happen? Should we rebel? Should we abandon God's word and risk going to Hell? This can't be our fate. What are the odds What are the chances? Are we to be punished by God or are we victims of circumstances?

From one generation to the next, all Londoners are cast down to the pits of heck. Beneath the swamp of pride is the pitfall of terror. When the fear of being abandoned becomes the fear of one's error, the fear of losing pride consumes the superior. Pride acts as a defence mechanism to prevent a schism – a division of belief between the expected and the actual – and, like an animal, we reinforce our defences. Hence, it is common sense. It is natural to act as we do. Scarred from earlier times, we are compelled to hide. We are concealed in society, hiding in plain sight, behind that pride, right?

So remove Him from his higher ground, for He's got nothing on me. A world without morals is the necessity. It's all about you, the bastard, being last to me. We ain't no bloody demons; we're just human beings. Look at our many faces of villain, seething beneath this hatred addiction. This is hidden behind a mask, so we ask for something else, all for the sake of our own damn health. But, between you and me, we truly believe, in the afterlife; that is, a life after this. We'll explain it to you all after, but you'll probably take the piss.

Be it Lord of the Holy or Lord of the flies, we're plagued with hope or marked with lies. We didn't fancy it, so we say 'fancy that', and like a prat, we were left in our own mess without an opinion, no less. So we confessed to God our thoughts; it left us defending ourselves in the courts. He judged our ways when we fell on our face. Still, we're men who can't be bought or sold down the river. Our soul had been delivered by the hands of fate; be it God or the demon. It might be real or perhaps we're dreaming or perhaps our imagination is running away like a heathen. In this woeful self-debate, we search for someone to loathe and we find someone to hate. But there's no one left to manipulate and no audience to view, so the foul soul of barren instils. If there's one lesson we learned from God, it's to never do as you're told, always fight and resist. Thank the Lord for giving us the ability to ball a fist.

Shanty X

♣

"A Shot Across the Bows"

THERE WERE NO NATURAL ANGLES IN THE WAY THEY BE SAILIN', and no gentle manners with which they were behavin'. Throughout the steaming clouds and tossing tides, a thick, green mass of Nature had arrived. Consuming the whole horizon from left to right ear, an enormous island through the vapour had appeared. The anchor was then released; we all felt it sink. As it hit hard and scarred the sandbar, we all had a drink. A sip of the ol' booze, a draught of the swill, a drop o' the ol' pure and another refill. The 'spirit' of the plant inside the scathed glass was consumed by men of the lowest class.

The sweetest smell of sandalwood allured their tongues and beaks, which drove motivation to dock at the white, sandy beach. As the aroma caressed their taste buds, it be replaced with the smell of shite; a rush of poignant body odour began to take flight. The crew, the lot of 'em, all abandoned their wits to cleanse the sweat from under their pits. Diving, jumping and running off the ship; all drunken sailors began to strip, so that they might replenish their appetite by consuming her secrets within these high tides. Hard labour and gin will save you from thinking, preventing you from cleaning your genitals and sin. They washed away at their dirty, little todgers, bathing and scrubbing each and every corner. Sweat came pouring from the skin of parts that don't see the light. The familiar sights and the sound of a seagull's mew allured them to a lighter blue. They passed coral by wading through aquatic creatures on the shores of Nauru.

And did them gorgeous lassies come greetin' our men, offering paniki, palm wine and green leaves of pandan.

Strange fruit, this, thought Thatcher, *But I'm starvin'!*

So he downed the lot without ever regardin'. There were smiles all round from those kind island folk, returned with grins hiding sins of the seafaring blokes. But without a word to state, Teefer could not communicate and thus his means to manipulate were no longer in play. No other brother could utter or mutter a stutter, except for Mr Gulliver, the most experienced mate. *I've been here before when my ship scraped the seafloor. These lands, I've explored, and I recognize this shore. I remember the natives were generous to me, when I Traded guns for food and other necessities.*

So, with that, Teefer removed his hat and bowed to and grinned to the Chief of the land. And since Mr Gulliver could speak the native tongue, Teefer used Gulliver, thus manipulation had begun.

With a few exchanges here and a few grins there, all became old pals. The pleasures that awaited them would elate the crew's morale. But, with no rationale, gluttony and indulgence replaced naïve kindness with malice and repugnance. To Prize's eyes, the tribesmen portrayed an applauding audience, satisfying fantasies stemming from a Narcissus complex. Then there was Thatcher, who'd been eyein' all the women, licking his lips at the Chief's daughter and her ripe pair of bosoms. Her breasts rippled from each and every motion, like the waves crashing in from the Ocean.

To complement the morning sunrise, the sun settled a palette in the skies. Paradise offered more than aquatica erotica. Magnificent innocence of the white beach assumed a state of exotica. Oils were refined from coconut flesh; the nuts ripened, then harvested, and all consumed the fresh. Water of the purest kind fell from the clouds, filtered by stone and earth, then draining into wells. Crystallized minerals formed in sheets of rock, which were used to decorate the Chief's livestock. Yet the men were not impressed with the beauties of Nature, and ridiculed the chief to show their displeasure.

A glimmer reflected light to the sinner, ensnared by the diamond and forming an image of the condemned. Amassed red transparency carved into a sphere, shaped by the Ocean's ebb and flow for a thousand years. The gem was perfect, pristine and crystal clear, and had absorbed all light and sound around, drowning all fear. Teefer gazed and marvelled at the precious piece, which had decorated the deserving, generous Chief.

But then he'd witness something peculiar in the stone; that familiar child, blissfully alone. Every man had become obsolete, and a single tear dropped down onto his dirt-stained feet. His memory melted away in the rain, as his mind's eye grew. The focus of rage caused the booze to ooze from his pores, and, with the claret, came an unhealthy smell of iron ore. Now sober and at peace with himself, he'd forgotten all his pride and regained his health. In that instant, betraying his instinct, the child inside would soon be ignored. He'd soon open fire on his new friendship, dissipating any shred of innocence.

Teefer felt obliged to confess his lie; he felt compelled to declare his decoy. He told an alternate story in order to deny how he was beaten as a young boy. This was the catalyst for his driving rage, yet the pride sunk in and he begun to behave like one of the rest of the lads in their cave – drinking themselves to death. 'Twas a man's escape. And so he told the men that he did not want to Trade, it was better to take by force and henceforth dominate.

What you see next is not what you'd expect; as Teefer turned his back, he faced his regret. His eyes rolled into the back of his head and his teeth ground slowly, like a lathe chipping lead. Some deep-seated role had begun to take hold; his emotions were unstable, yet still rather bold. A spark would ignite the fight between God and his right-hand man. And here in the sand God had become the one abandoning the Holy land. The remaining survivor was the Devil himself, waiting on His right shoulder, like a doll on a shelf. A whisper he would obey, to victimize and betray, or to sabotage and pillage his prey.

There's no time for the fresh and fruitful. I be seekin' something more useful. D'y'ave me any booze to warm me cockles? I've the Devil's appetite from that lady in the bottle. I've no care for these petty treats, for me teeth be favourin' a flavour; a drop of the ol' sweet. His eagerness swallowed his weakness, as he devoured a bottle of gin in one sitting.

Rapiers, cutlasses and sabres, unsheathed by the slavers. As the translation came through, not a moment too soon, a frowning chief became the outcast, which didn't last because he was soon blasted by the bastard. A loose shot escaped, demonstrating their ruthlessness. Gunpowder blew a hole through the unwise and toothless. *The chief be needin' a good bullet to the heart; he'd be bleedin' from his guts bein' all torn apart.*

A tingling in the spine had been bleaching the rind of all the members of the chief's tribe. What then happened immediately followed; all glee had been replaced with remorseful sorrow. In fear of the man with the crooked teeth, Teefer's club joined in the murdering of the chief. The tribesmen complied for Teefer was omnipotent. All works of the bay, even the wise and innocent, were in control of this immigrant. 'Twas a state of imprisonment for the dissonant dissident.

Shanty xi

♥

Personal Violence

COME ONE, COME ALL; GATHER ROUND CHILDREN, WE'VE GOT SOMETHING FOR you all. Watch us brawl in the boxing ring. Treat your lassies and have a pint to drink. Watch as we be masculinity. Watch as we bleed out in this fight, protecting our might, so you might not think otherwise. Walk right into my hanging fists, like the rest of the herd. It's givin' me the propa hump, this; indeed, in splendid fervour. No further than the rest of you beasts who come trampled, just as well. One smack in his gob will send them all straight to Hell. This ain't no straightforward task. There's no method that would outlast the fastest lout. So you'd better drink up and get out. For it's way past the hour of the night, and the fight is now lost by the most glorious King. It took us years to get here; now it's lingering. All the drunken punters showed no sense of dignity and no originality; no speculation, specifically in its entirety.

To hell with him; off my thoughts for life. He wronged us somehow, so now we ignore his background; we stare at his mug, for we wanna see that thug. We wanna know what a cunt looks like. As if a gander at a man with this interference will alleviate our anguish, depending on his appearance. We look over our shoulder before we slag him off. It's one quick glance round the shop before we tell him to piss off. Have a look round before drowning the clown. Give him a warning before ignoring the wrongdoing and belt him one now. The coast is clear to thump him in the ear, and we all get away with it every year. We hide in the darkness and hunt him. We follow his every mood, from sneer to grin. We pounce on the victim when the time is right; a fist in his right eye to rob the cunt blind.

Who's to authorize the authoritative punter? You acted as the hero of the day. For when we punched that cunt in the face, the copper came to your parade. And we suppose we're the villain in your fairy tale, as you planted your anger on us like a bloody target. We wouldn't have started this if you lot weren't such pricks. Now we're bleeding from the mouth, left alone without the louts. You won't get the satisfaction from me, only a senseless fantasy. And we walk away from your society in our realistic state of reality. That's what you think, its plain and clear. The state is painted on your expression; we can see it from here.

We can't help these cards we've been dealt. Wrong doings are brewing from the way we have felt. You give us no credit, so we edit ourselves; after which we regret it. And we've said it to you time and time again; five times over, 'till we're weak and sober. Now we feel like we can't give over no more, as we ring your bell and knock on your door. And still the pride has the priority over the brutality of our bloody hands. We feel the flow of the blood in strips, dripping in the sand. We feel the raw carnage, so we attempt to harness the pulp, neglecting the recognition of that guilt in our gulp.

We be painted-faced heathens with not much left to eat. We be left there to starve in the streets, picking for bones to satiate the feed. There're bits and pieces of muscle in the stew, the origins of which no one knew. A flash of bone and blood come running through the conveyor belt of the mental room. Gore's occupyin' too many cogs, 'n' there's not much space left for the ol' noggin. And the thug in us will surely display itself, ever so evidently; no mare is there to care or resurrect me. Leaking wretched recollections and hiding behind the hate, we once witnessed the beheading and hanging of our closest mate. When the rope tightens, the neck may break, emitting a sound that perturbs. When the head comes rolling off that stage, those children become disturbed.

Smother another clod of mud to camouflage the lot. The soft tissue is nothing when she's dead. The eyes roll in the back of her head in which emotion lacks. Nature doesn't stare back. Starving 'till the cheeks fall off the bone, like meat from a cleaver. The life is sucked out from the nasty scarlet fever. The deprived man bolsters his image by destroying the environment around him. These are just few examples of the stories on our streets. Plenty more stories will be coming soon round here, but never to those elites.

SHANTY XII

♦

"SHAKE A LEG"

THE IGNITION OF THE END HAD FLARED OUT, IMPLODING; rolled back onto itself; and, in an instant, somehow, a flame came into existence. Wood channelled it ripe; a carved tool for the ol' burn. There be the man with his pipe, smoking by the stern. Blowin' rings before whistling a familiar tune, that once was sung by a soddin' buffoon. He'd a mind with time to unwind.

And just then did that man catch a thought – a premonition. Caught by the entanglement of like-minds between himself and his twin. An ethereal connection hiding in disguise, he envisions Mr Guido victimized by his own device, thereby painting a lucid and horrendous image behind Gulliver's eyes.

Simultaneously, on the forward side of the vessel, Guido had begun to experiment with his handmade chemicals. After much focus and careful revision, he prepared each sample, testing various conditions. One by one, he then set each alight, recording reporting as each began to ignite. Coconuts with gunpowder applied had erupted, spitting fragments of hide, and forcing flesh and milk from the inside to make a mess on the decks' starboard side. But one of these little beauties had not erupted like the rest. It had been sitting on the edge of the ship; a dud, no less. After waiting impatiently for several dismal moments, Guido in frustration grabbed the one seemingly broken, and rattled it with his open hands. The heat of friction in combination with the sun had smoked and relit the primer, thus the process had begun. Slamming the coconut onto the floor, Guido then booted the blighter as if she were his own whore.

Let us now remember that, prior to their embarkment, Guido hid a black substance within his hosiery compartment. His anger fuelled an inability to remember hiding it in his sock. Unlike his twin, who had foreseen this paradox, Guido was blind to his own gunpowder plot. The last munition and the remnants of the powder blasted Guido's foot right off, causing a sound much louder. Without comprehension, the loud bang caught everyone's attention. And did them men come running right over to witness and feel the tension.

On all fours and restless on the floor, glistening flesh was hanging out and more. He did not scream; he became quite silent until he realized his own act of violence. To keep his glosso from being gnawed, a hard piece of wood was placed between his jaws. And now the pain could be released – concentrated in the grinding of teeth. To control the bleeding, Gulliver applied a compression device beneath Guido's right knee. Still in agony and with a bang in the gob to knock him spark out, Guido continued to sob and moan. Gulliver, though rather skilled he, was not strong enough to saw through the bone. So it was asked of Mr Thatcher to continue the incision with brute force alone, yet without Gulliver's precision. The medical procedure ended with a sharp snap; a disturbing sound that echoed in the minds of each lad. Now that the pain did intensify, Guido's face be mortified. The impulsive thought of fear came as his imagination was triggered by the sound ringing in his ear. His eyes became tight; the vessels constricted. His body convulsed in seizure and weakened. Soaked in spirit, cauterized by flame, losing his right foot, he had only himself to blame. No sympathy came from the lads as the poor bugger fainted, for each of 'em watchin' over were rather selfish and tainted. All except Gulliver, who shared this sibling bond; he gazed into Guido's eyes, searching for a response. But Guido had not died, as the men had all thought. He'd been restin' his eyes to escape the feeling of distraught.

Over the next few moments, there was much debate of Gulliver's prophetic omens and Guido's dying fate. No compassion came from Bill Blyth, who'd offered to end Guido's life, with a quick thrust from the blade of his knife. *To end our morale suffering throughout my crew, one swift blow to his gullet will do!*

As a result of Bill's scheme, Gulliver tried to advise Mr Teefer in his cabin, offering a compromise. However,

Teefer did not consider the request of Mr Gulliver, he only minded the choice of words that Bill had uttered: *Throughout my crew; how dare he!* And, with that, Teefer approved of Gulliver's plea. This did not set well with Bill the K'nniver, who'd no sympathy for his brothers, as he was a schemin' blighter who'd be cheatin' all the others. So as long as old man was standing by his side, Teefer – the chief manipulator – could sense the blade of the knife.

All men were in silence; apart from Guido, who was still agonized. There was no hope for survival, for these migrants lacked medical supplies. Without disinfectant and proper care, no attempts could be made to alleviate Guido's despair.

Alone, the brothers gaze through each other's eyes. Unspoken, with true colours, the brothers unite in foresight. A vow of silence precedes the inevitable ending of Guido's life. Stained with cracked blood and covered in mud, those filthy hands smother the runt. He be pleadin' while he be bleedin' thick all over the wooden deck soon to receive no sympathy from those cursed ones in heck. And he be like the beggar with eyes wide open; so sincere in his request, but still no bugger would mind the shite who'd now became depressed. His life was gone, but what is life? A force of Nature struggling to survive. A story in itself, read by no mortal sod; a life is read by only Him, be it Jack or be it God.

♠ ♣ ♥ ♦

As the match had struck the rough, an ignition had flared out above, imploding, rolling back onto itself and, in an instant, somehow, a flame came. There be the man with his pipe, smoking by the bow and ripened from the previous inhale. Clothes smelled of cold smoke, this bloke. *The ol' burn, mind you, calms the blood.*

Caught by the foresight mentioned the night before. And, like a whore, she changed her flow, ploughing straight into the bow where Gulliver had been hangin' around. So he dropped his tool like a drunken fool, spillin' out the fibres from within. Orange and blacky, along with the baccy, set a fire for the ol' Mr Satan.

A bulge of baccy sparked, landing on its mark; the remnants of black grain, caused a chain reaction. A fraction of dirt flirted with a trail that would be the end of the ship and the males on board. Yet this was all foreseen in the twins' shared vision, provoking Gulliver to make a decision. Should he take his own life, to save the rest of mankind alike? Should he deviate from the hate, from the unnatural flow? Should he behave himself, act as the hero?

To prevent this all from happening, Gulliver coated himself with kerosene and proceeded to the bow of the boat to amend his vow; he'd have one last smoke. His body in a bone fire scorched the flesh black behind red flames. The pristine white teeth of a charred corpse would be seen beneath. All men watch as the hero dies, changing from red to black, then ash, then flies.

Shanty XIII

♠

Skint

THE POOR'VE GOT NOTHING TO LOSE, SO WHY NOT LET THE RICH TAKE IT ALL. Have a ball at our expense. Take the bleedin' lot, go on; sell it to your fence. What scraps you have left, sell for anything you can get – no shillings, only pence. And hence we shall take our earnings to the fullest extent. Gents, let's have a bet. He's holding all the cards. He's singing like a bard. He has the sweetest of treats, oh bless his heart. Love or loathe, you choose your mode of emotion for that lovely rogue. Be it the man in vogue or the snivelling toad, the choice is yours on that highwayman's crossroad. How it's framed depends on whether you're game. Depending how they like to play depends on how I behave.

Can't help it to be dealt with the way we were born; those elite defeat our ego in scorn. Robbed me at youth from here to the cradle, fuelling their egos with false self-appraisal. With four pompous brows all scarred, they browse and stare at us real hard. Lasting impression all fast, and we recommend they leave, before our fists break their perfect teeth. We recommend them to be removed before this punch breaks their perfect tooth. I walk up and down around the town with a frown – my smile upside down. There's no sympathy and no empathy, only pity for me; where is my crown? I just stare at the ground in shame, though there's no one to blame 'cept my own soddin' name.

All the youth are aberrant fools, so every man must find his tool. You must contribute to society how you see fit, despite the tight chains wrapped around our contained wrists. If we keep these traditions enforced, then men are inevitably oppressed, yet all this hard, manly labour will grow hairs on your chest. And those elites never learnt to give an ear to the crying streets, which dared to shed tears in exchange for bloody meat. So, place yourself in the flames and let the flow of the fire drain you from your wits. Go on, have another pint to drink.

A thousand years of pride, built from the salt on our hides. A torque of metal stretches the marks on your hands. Never mind, watch them gauges. Twelve-hour shifts on this platform on which we stand; all of which is a cinch for men in the industrial ages. Sweat rolls and runs off the bleeders, as each man works by pulling them levers. Iron grinds crumbling rock through this makeshift mechanism. Puddles all around dirty feet ripple from the dripping clouds, disturbing their own reflection. Black smoke smears the sky blue into cobalt, by default. The city is dressed in industry; rivers consume rivets and bolts.

Characteristic of man's dismay, yet, in essence, 'tis simply man-made. Cobblestone moss remained for decades, brick'll turn black from years of grey, left there solid to remain 'till war breaks. Soot smudges feet when toes walk the beat. There are too many faces with their ugly mouths to feed. There's no need to leave, when the spoils are here; my greed'll feed me when we down that lovely beer. Payday has arrived; I shan't share with the wife. We'll pop round to the pub to get sloshed, we'll be there by eight o' clock.

The toll of labour spits out; it's cold, bleak and frosty. Driving urges become old, weak and rusty. And then there's me, all bitter and sullen at the upper levels of the gents that rule and govern. Conform in uniform, be complimentary. To the King we beg, who's constantly condescending me. That be me last of hearts, merely bruised and swollen; 'tis but me pride bein' manipulated and stolen. With banter, we may disguise ourselves in tongue, whether we're sober or drunk, to protect ourselves from the elites. We be the defendant; they be the judge. And so let the grime on our teeth make us gain motivation. Let the sharp angles around our eyes remind the high how to recognize.

Recognize the dirt between our toes; they're no different than the sludge under our shoes, and no better than the holes in our clothes. We pong of old, stale brine; our leathers reek of dried urine. That be the stereotype of swine. Excrete in the mud and cleanse with the same; roll around like a thug, covered in muddy stains. These stains on materials made us less competent, less corroborative and less consistent, yet more persistent. Adopting manners of the peasant is not so pleasant, yet contributes to the present situation.

We peasants take out our aggression and butcher the pig into meat, soaked in blood and mud; 'twas a pleasant peasant's feast. 'Twas a stroke of luck for the week, now we be nourished from tasty pig's feet. Compiled from pooling our resources, what little scraps we had. We had no other option but to force feed our gob with left over chops stolen from the local butcher's shop, so that we could continue to direct our voice towards the lack of choice.

In all this working-class isolation, you'll see how proud people are of their deprivation. The rulers want law and prosperity, but the rebels just keep having children without maturity. In the great battle between chaos and order, the atrophies spill over the rim, across the border. They cut every corner, like fleeing little rats, to attain what little leverage they have over the aristocrats. But no methods seems to work, and they're trying their 'ardest; they're abandoned their children, who have now become bastards.

"So you wander through each charter'd street, near where the charter'd Thames still flows, and witness the marks in each and every face you meet, marking weakness and woe. In every cry of every man, and, in an instant, an infant cries in fear. In every voice on this British land, the mind-forged manacles we hear. How the chimney sweep's cry every black'ning church applauds; and the hopeless soldier's sigh runs in blood down those palace walls. But, mostly, through the midnight streets we hear how the whores curse, blasting a newborn's naïve tears and blights with plagues the marriage hearse."[3]

---

3   Adopted from 'London' by William Blake.

SHANTY XIV

♣

"THE CUT OF HIS JIB"

A LITTLE BEAUTY WOULD APPEAR AMONG THE CLOUDS AND SEA, arriving at the shores of Fiji. No one had grasped the notion of throwing the corpse into the Ocean. No one could face this heroic act; it soothed them more to ignore this fact. Morale was low, nonetheless, but not because of the rotting flesh. 'Twas because they all had a craving for booze, no less. You see, soon after a man dies do those other men become paralyzed by sippin' on that lovely brew, downing the lot and leaving none for you. But the problem was that they were all tapped out; all of the booze had soon run out. Faces all round had turned a malnourished hue: a mix of pale beige and morbid sky blue. 'Twasn't until they stood their ground that the hue flashed back to pink all round.

A wretched ire had begun to unravel, so it was no surprise that gossip would evaluate the tension; not to mention the potential mutiny. And where was the booty on this Black Beach? It seems like a load of old cobblers, if you ask me. But as the crew's chief clerk, I have no objection. I just write it all down, 'tis my speculation.

Another trick was up his sleeve, as Teefer began to weave a concoction of mead. Gluts and gluts of coconuts were amassed by shaking trees, to fulfil Thatcher's guts and the rest of the SOBs. He'd be distillin', learning from scratch, to satisfy the urges of that Mr Thatch. From a puff of the ol' burn, Teefer had delivered; he had kindled a fire, to remove one's hearts from those aching shivers. Absorbing the balance between the Trades of the two, and learnin' to forget the past to create the new you.

So there he was, boiling milk of the coconut in a vessel made of glass, conduits and whatnot. A tube of intestine was used to trap the fluid to ingest. Droplets of ale collected in a chamber, thinning the blood, bile and other bodily flavours. The prototype was complete – a successful masterpiece: the epitome of the others' work from the perished fleet. Even the old man was especially impressed with Mr Teefer's triumphant attempt. Mass production had soon begun, but without the aid of a resource plan. The day had come to quench the throat; all hands on deck, gathering supplies from the boat. All except Thatcher, who'd wandered off. He blurted out some drivel before buggering off. But all the other men who were left behind had a dry tongue, and thus a goal in mind. So, there they were, all workin' to the core. Following instructions like one of Jack's whores. All the peasants and sycophants alike crowded together to discuss the latest strife. While the

King sat all alone, with no other to match his status, no other understood his pain, neither God nor the latter.

♠ ♣ ♥ ♦

The bright colours of the day merged with the sky; azure consumes all. Sea winds rolled and folded between two blues mirrored, reminding them all of that missing bigot. But there be plenty of liquor to disregard despair and still no word of Thatcher, yet no blighter cared. *He can handle himself; he doesn't need any help.*

A few hours here and a few drinks there, and they became rather pissed. The sun began to set and their friend was sorely missed. The azure sky turned to navy while the remaining light made their vision hazy. To inspire more colour, some light be required. With little kerosene left to burn, wax candles were lit; it was an everlasting scene, described beautifully and romantic. Yet their grins still remained, concealing the pain, and casting impressions of their faces to hide any remaining truth and hesitations. The shadows from the flame whispered and flickered over their wicked grins, painting scars marked with gold in the dark; 'twas an archaic method of art.

Currency comes in many forms; disguising truth for power was the norm. And in this social hierarchy, Teefer created a monopoly, with Prize and Bill on the same platform. The last in line were old man and the childe, who were forced to explore the jungle and shore. Old man was new to this area, yet inferred what he had learnt from the prior. Along the way, old man had told many tales about Trade and all his escapades. You see, old man had always known what was lying beneath the throne and by his own form of prose, leaving no stone unturned, old man implicitly told the childe all about Teefer and his guile. *Fact portrayed as fiction is the best form of diction to depict a man of contradiction.*

As the childe began to listen and acknowledge, the pair soon approached an item glistening through the foliage. From then on, their course changed. For each step made, the foot was carefully placed. The sound of cracking twigs was replaced with rustling; so subtle, yet still restless. Nevertheless, they proceeded to the entrance to eavesdrop, unbeknownst to their guests. There be Mr Thatcher tied to a tree, surrounded by painted-faced heathens calling out in a frenzy. The tribesmen caterwauled and howled at the smile facing his scowl. Faced with the sharp end of his own cutlass, buried deep into the buttress, gluts and gluts of coconuts came spewin' from his ragged guts. The pain on Eddie's large face sent shivers down the spine that one could taste. 'Twould make you sick to the stomach to witness that bigot. Tied like a lummox, no rest for the wicked. 'Twould make ya skin turn green, like rottin' flesh. 'Twould make ya hairs stand up on the back of ya neck. 'Twould make you feel sympathy for this Goliath in heck. And, sadly, in the end, all will inevitably forget.

All watched this dreadful scenario 'cept Prize, that handsome Lothario. Approach that tribe did he so smugly, so that he might take a chance, to lure the men with his charm. For he had overpowering wittiness that delighted the tribesmen in a matter of seconds, but not before Eddy had been left headless. Did them tribesmen come pouring into the world of their new Captain. Praising at his feet like their prophesized messiah, for Prize had deceived them all, naturally, like a cunning liar. Prize had achieved what Eddie could not, since Eddie was only muscle, insignificant to that lot. So Eddie's head rolled down the mound heaped from the ground, bumping into several trees, before tumbling into the crowd of SOBs. A game of Shrovetide football caused by neglect sent Eddie's head over the edge of the ledge, and there it went down the descent and thumped into the Ocean, plummeting to the bottom, sinking and drowning in slow motion.

At that point in time, the tribe had treated Prize to some of Eddie's meat. And, with a kind of amusement, he refused politely the taste of the sweet. Just then did Prize gloat by showing his golden teeth to the members of the boat. Now for the first time, the chief manipulator eyed Prize in a specific light, as no different from the rest of his guests, not even Bill the Knife. The chief manipulator had now recognized Prize as potential threat. Prize was an avid gambler, always havin' a bet. But now, at Teefer's expense, his actions he would soon regret.

SHANTY XV

♥

SWEET HARLOTS

T HOSE LACKING SCRUPLES VIEW THE NEWEST DRAMA AS RATHER useful. These mild attacks are there to distract; we find them appealing and they're there to attract. These are the ingredients that make this world revolve. Women are always looking for a puzzle to solve. Round 'em all up before they all escape. Pound her rounds and take; rough her up a bit, 'till the circle loses its shape. Destroy her in our domain 'till she becomes tame. She'll submit, be passive and admit we're massive. If you must, we won't make a fuss. We confess that this contest is no longer just. So we force our lust on her bust; as she screams out Wilde's name, we shall violently thrust.

That be Ms Lyon, who once made a nice little earner by breaking her hymen. Broken into from multiple phalli penetrating through, her body went into visceral déjà vu. She could've been the perfect wife, but now she's too bruised.

The biological aspects of sex kill the mental aspects of love, like the hunter firing an arrow into a pure white dove. It is not good enough for either of us or for every woman, we are aware. Nor can we match them exactly in their trust; nor do we worry, nor do we care. We have assumed them honest, but, in the end, they were caught. Women come under my wing, or so we thought. We never asked for anything in return, nor did they offer. We asked for that special favour, but next time we shan't bother. All we can do is to steal it back. What choice had they left us? What choice do we have?

All it took was one argument, and now she's back on the streets, sellin' herself in regret and admitting self-defeat. Desperate to be beneath the sheets of any other SOB, she finds her way upstairs towards our door as we stand there proudly.

Oh please, sir. I beg you, she says so pathetically. *May I enter your bed? I'll do anything you say.*

We were amazed and blown away that the logic had impossibly escaped. There was absolutely no way we could begin to explain or convey the mayhem. Ladies among these men will always be a rarity in this idealized social scheme. How could we reject such a sweet offer which captures our attention span? How can we refuse her proffer? For we are only a man. So, we take her under our wing so that she can sing to our sins and praise us for all o' our wins. We often go to the Lyon's Den, so she can cheer us on. She stays with us 'till the night is over and all the punters have gone. She's rather fortunate to be ours, as we provide her wine. We beat her when she's running the gob; she is our concubine.

Sympathetic is so pathetic when you got the lust from deep below the gut. A love for the naked is a bond for the hatred. You gotta be nasty, for it won't starve me. If we don't make a fuss we can't crave for the lust. You got what you wanted, but what about us? What we want is always what we need. It ain't greedy; it's our survival. In this search, we will find a companion – our rival. The fat and muscle, you call it flesh. Grab it as you please, as man knows best. Like plucking the apple from the vine, the apple needs to be plucked; it's like the body of a virgin who needs to make love.

These women, they're hurt by the fantasy of men. And, these men, they drink away an idea that one day they might've been a legend. We all doubt you'll disagree when we say, *Believe me*. We choose to live in own fantasy that one day scholars will read about us in vast libraries, as they explore the world of thievery. So we are merely laying out the legacy for the future of our country.

What I need is always what I want, because we live in a society of selfish cunts. Male and female. Predator and prey. One takes command as the other disobeys. But today is your lucky day to give way to the tyranny. Give us your face, your smile and your dignity. The walls of the virgin torn down with an opening. It starts with a gathering and then she starts to sing. A word or two can leave your flesh hanging rather in bloom and soon it will be more people in the room to share it with you.

Without an ounce of courage, we bring you the filth and we bring to you the rubbish; it's not worth anything lavish, 'tis but shoddy disparage. So what's left of the marriage with Ms Lyon, a whore? Broken into for so much more. Those ladies we seek; those ladies we adore. What do we have to do to get her preggers? She'll be up the duff tonight, then we'll forget her. Lady of the night and lady of the day. Lady won't want to behave until we gives her the pay. So we agrees and we shall proceed. We cave to get access to her tray of treats below her waist and above her knees. 'Twas sour but sweet; a feast for the beast.

Being too drunk to remember that special night in November, getting their names all wrong. This cheeky lad (who could use a smack) had a habit of calling everyone John. More witty than true nothings, whose value is openly made. Float around in social spheres, ending the night on the green grass blade. Gazin' at the stars shootin' through the air, while she be playin' kindly with our dirty, black chest hair. She be singin' in our ear, like an angel's harp, 'till we spoil the mood by letting loose a pard'. And there was she, leanin' on me wallet, that be Black-eyed Sally and me gazin' at the comets.

Shanty XVI

◆

"Like Rats Deserting a Sinking Ship"

T HE GLASS EYE OF BILL THE KNIFE MADE IT CLEAR THAT HE appeared like the devil inside. While Prize's gold teeth led you to believe he was your mate, but really you were his bait.

You can never understand the plan, says Bill the Knife with a blade inside. *Keep myself with all the secrets? Would I lie? And if I did, would you believe it?* Bill never looked Teefer in the eye when he gave him the alibi. Nor did Teefer gaze upon Prize's grin while he been stealin' some more of Teefer's gin. A written note was left there, pinned with a knife to the cabin door of our Captain. Only one such swindler had such a signature. The printed side had

73

been blackened with tobacco soot, which already began to come off and soiled from boots; the blank side had been written with the same substance. I'll never forget that dreadful sentence:

The man with the hat gets a knife in the back.

The design was written, signed in blood and singed with flame. 'Twas a bold attempt, lacking the option to relent and repent. Underneath this curtain was the shell of truth. There it was, dripping the club of gents dry, so that he may try to pry it open with another cruel joke, that bloke. Each member of his audience may be the enemy. Let him entertain the crowd with the story of the Black Beach and, after that, let another stab him in the back. Still, there is a certain level of diplomacy when you can only approximately feel the truth.

That night, below deck, as men placed their bets on Teefer's neck, Teefer felt the paranoia. Imagine that knife piercing a tiny hole in the neck of our employer. All punters, with their made-up faces, were laughing while Teefer was sulking alone in the shadows. Have a shave and place the blade on his throat, while quenching his whiskers with whisky. Eventually, he did agree and arrive late in the night, only to find the boys drinking all his wine. No bugger bothered to utter or stutter a plea.

But, here, have some o' me ol' grog, which I've mixed with rum, spice and tea. So Teefer proceeded to take the vessel and, to some degree, believed the hyperbole.

Hold on now, my dearest lad, interjected Prize. *I don't think you can trust this man we all call 'Bill the Knife'. He wrote that soddin' letter; I seen it with my own two eyes. He drinks your brandy to get his throat wetter; he's the devil to demonize. Should you let him be, you are likely to jeopardize all our lives, since no one can trust a culprit in this enterprise.* With those remarks, Knife be stigmatized, and the crew embarked, leaving Bill behind.

Prize had kept his plans to himself in his head, while reassuring Teefer that he was ahead. Prize had concealed this deceptive ruse, while Teefer be distracted by his ego and booze. All except old man believed in Prize's lies, since he'd witnessed him writing the note on the previous night. Yet he was not in the position to accuse the young man, for he had no speech and no respect from this savage clan. So he kept this in mind, continuing to watch over the players and evaluating the men in this game of betrayal.

Since no soul on board was magnanimous, the ultimate choice was unanimous. All sought to hold down Bill, while each took turns beating the bleeder. They tied him up and cast him out, anticipating booting him from the crowd. No one 'cept old man and childe stepped down. The Knife's lack of persuasion was not part of the equation. In the eyes of the few, Bill was no longer a member of the commune, and in the afternoon Bill was to be marooned. The remaining five would be Teefer, old man, childe, myself and Prize; the rest of the crew had either left or died.

'Twas Prize's claim and therefore duty to constrain Bill to the root of a tree; there he would remain for eternity, preventing a potential mutiny. Bill be dragged by a rope tied around his neck and dragged to a hill, away from the deck. He stumbled to follow, his feet dragging in the sand. Prize's soul was hollow, but his ego was grand. For he had expelled his rival to ensure his survival, while Knife was shamed in defeat, hence his draggin' feet. Neither of the brothers would utter nor mutter a stutter to one another because both knew their place. No words of worth penetrated the masterminds; 'twas once written on their faces, but 'twas now left behind.

There'd only be a few words from Prize to Bill; 'twould be just the two men on the top of the hill. *Don't you just love pushing the man on top? Don't you just want to see him fall on the floor, so we can spit on his crawl? Elitist is his weakness, his poverty and his shame and now comes your moment to debase the blighter's name.*

Yet Mr Blyth could no longer think; he had no bottle – nothing left to drink. Once deprived of his bravery, man is left to slavery. It took a long time before becoming aware, tense fingers wrapped around his bare, trapping the flow of bloody red. His fingernails scraped off skin, passing over blue veins and red lines on the other side. A wicked cry unleashed on prey, only releases once weak and maim. Accumulating the hate lends itself to the innate, returning to the Wilde streak that we all crave.

And, so, there you have it: Prize's confession. Let that be a lesson. At no other moment will we hear Prize mentioning his true intentions, for his was the underlying manipulation built on pride and wit. It is Prize who is the foundation and Teefer as his counterfeit.

Scars from the sorrow, my dearest fellow in-arms; arms in need as we partake in protecting the boss's greed. Watch and learn, and we feed ourselves with scraps of meat thrown by the man on the throne.

A subtle smile and a volte-face will leave the triumphant one with all the class, and leave the shamed one stripped of his brass as a single drop o' grog pours from his glass. His pride was closed, yet it was pried open by a more cunning rogue who riled and roped him.

As Blyth's hollow body remained, with no code to abide by, thin strips of water began to fall from the sky. The crew went on board and just stood by, while a tear rolling down began to crack Blyth's glass eye. Just as all men thought they were home and dry, the wind and pressure began to amplify. It was all hands on deck to prep and set sail, full speed ahead to let the gallant beat the gale.

It was a rising wall of water that intimidated the spectre of the soul in the bravest of men, chillin' the bones of all on board our humble ship. The wall was the strength of God Himself, which no human being could ever contend with, and we all knew it from the shallow tears in our eyes to the deepest pit of our minds. At that moment, the wave came crashing down, sweeping in with so much force that our desperation was silenced. It came down on our prayers to a God we ignored and down on our permanent collective pride. We submit our bodies as they become flaccid, controlled by the sea. But at least she has us in her ardent arms, whispering in our ears all of her secrets until we consume too much and discover our own ends. We are innocent, we are children; we are foolhardy to think otherwise. It is true that only when we die, do we release all that pride. And the underlying feelings becomes the purest, like on the day we were born.

Shanty XVII

♠

Childhood

'Twas the very eve of Treason Day; fire scorched bone, turning flesh and the resulting death into flame. A thick smog lifted to blacken the skies. There were all sorts of colours in the night; 'twas a magical sight. We remember the smell of burning oak, smoke so thick it could startle a choke. And the char on the throat was no different than the breath of dust when breaking the coal; 'twas a child's must, which made you whole. We remember all too well what happened on that night. Come see into that child's eyes and see what it's like.

You look into that child's eyes and wonder if he's to suffer. Will he be starved? Will he continue to feel hunger? Will those tiny arms strain from back-breaking labour? Will his black eyes be stained by the trampling boot, from the dusty coal or from leftover soot? How long will his body resist decline from malnourishment? The dirt absorbs the juicy flesh and soon dries the core to brown, and quickly that child will be worn down. This is the process of learning to age; alongside the experience comes the drive of rage. Smiling makes one vulnerable to the pending ridicule of those around, so those children must still their mouths. Make no peep, not one sound.

A prize, a guinea, a pound, a crown, a few pennies less – there's not too many goin' round. It be the way to proceed with a mother in need, but it's not the life for me. What we want is never what we need, so we learnt to thieve; we think you'd all agree. When pretending like a child, the pretender becomes an actor; the adoption of an identity is a common human factor. Manipulation comes by acting this role – pretending to be confident and pretending to be bold. This we learnt, not from the old, since father left us, or so we were told. We learnt it from the streets, by watching other tea leaves givin' false stories while they be picking from their marked target's sleeves. And this control was thrilling; 'twere me first earnin' of a shilling. Some boys like violence, but others enjoy winning.

Without a soul, there's no desire for contemplation. Much be easy to ignore in this role; no notes are ever taken. But there be one night that we can never ignore. That be one Treason Day, at the young age of four. On that particular night, men without common sense nabbed and nicked a bottle of wine, cheese and a loaf of bread. Standing there ready and waiting in suspense, guilty as was plainly seen. Several hangings were to commence for men of poor hygiene. One of whom were a familiar face, who we'd dined with and shared grace. 'Twasn't the lager that started it all, but 'twas the father of mine who'd began my downfall. We used to be good boy, but the sights broke our spirit. All those public executions turned us into a selfish bigot. We watched me father hang there with me mother at side, as his neck was broken in a blink of an eye. But to this very day, did me mother deny the death of me father, who'd made me a bastard and caused me to get plastered as life passed me by.

To commemorate his legacy, we were encouraged to take up carpentry; like father before me, and the father before him, we learnt the craft and took a liking to gin. After many years of this trade, we got largely bored, so we picked up a new profession; 'twas larceny to which we explored. Now let us negotiate appropriately, so that we may renovate emotionally, and I shall remove myself from all responsibility – the burden of society.

At age twelve, a boy becomes a man. For this is the time we roam the land. Then there's me, all proud and laughing, seduced by a whore desperate for a farthing. This moment captures the new Jack Trade, whom we all have grown to love. Reflecting back to our youth, when angels were sent from up above.

With manhood comes the game of drunken banter to show 'em all your special flavours, boasting with witty answers. This skill was mastered quite early on, bolstering my local reputation. There in the Lyon's Den was a new crowd of faces to listen to our poetic tongue, voicing devilish phrases. So there be the basics; me early days were not so abrasive as one might have placed them. There was no abuse to go on my behalf; in fact, my raising was a ruddy good laugh.

SHANTY XVIII

♣

"SHOWING HIS TRUE COLOURS"

COMPLEX IS A DEVELOPED MULTITUDE OF IMPOSED PERSONAS built on a foundation of pride. The only secrets men maintain become the greatest lie. Hidden attributes swim in an Ocean of many other available attributes. Yet the only retrieved attributes are the most superficial, and the essential attributes are buried in the deep.

The squall kisses a question into the Ocean, and the crashing waves revealed her answers. If you listen carefully to one of those crashing waves you may momentarily awake, thus acknowledging that you have based your whole life on this lie. Somewhere deep in the cognitive mechanisms of the mind, the true self is within, drowning in an Ocean of attributes. White light and silence for a while. No sense of sight, but a sense of violation. There are no stimuli and no sounds to hear. Something controls this impending doom, yet nothing controls the sense of fear. Will I grasp onto reality or will I soon slip back into this dream?

You recognize nothing, yet you cannot recall how to recognize. In this state you are void, but – as you recognize this fact – you begin to harmonize with the tangible. You open your eyes to a view of changing colours in the sunset, between clouds and the sea. Corporal sensations remind us that we are not just conscious beings, but humans in need of water. You crawl in the sand like a worm, searching in dirt 'till you feel the spitting of the crashing waves relieving the hurt.

Mangled metal and timber chips were the only remains of the ruined ship destroyed by the storm the night before, scathing rocks against the shore. There be the crew all battered and scattered around the coastline, their tongues dehydrated with the taste of sea brine. One eye follows another, and the third began to consider the scene of reality.

♠ ♣ ♥ ♦

The sleeves of Prize began to pry open, as he lay there facing away from the Ocean. The chief manipulator could not manage to manipulate the old man and childe, and struggling to persuade his right-hand man, who be Prize, with a coy smile. Prize turns his back to face the young and old, so that he would have his audience to influence and control. Teefer stood fast, displaying his crooked teeth, yet Prize returned to his accuser, claiming he was the Knife's sheath. But with no words from the old and young, Prize turned boldly to expose his tongue. A bright, golden shine was emitted from Prize's canines, lavishing rays of gold to saturate his audience's pride. No words could teefer utter to express his defeat. Prize was the man who, admittedly, could not be beat. But old man knew about Prize's foundation. Old Man knew he was the devil in decoration and with teefer's silence, Old Man assumed manipulation, then he would assume conscious dictation.

Old Man exposed Prize's lies to emphasize teefer's position. Prize scoffed and ignored the Old Wise Man's accusation, claiming to have no proof, only false allegations. The Wise defeated Prize without physical persuasion, sending Prize to his own damnation. Old Man did not manipulate his opponents with deception or tricks, but instead by building premises through questions; Old Man relied on logic.

Old Man introduced himself as Robin the Great Crusader, and explained he was unable to speak before, being drowned by the crew's harsh behaviour. You see, the Old Wise Man does not speak, but observes. Until the time is right, his thoughts are reserved. He conceals his wisdom to those who listen such as the young childe and men on a mission. In the presence of lads, Old Man was outranked. He kept silent until his wisdom would be thanked.

Following a brief gentlemen's game and a swift puff of our pipes, the Wise Man told his story when the time became ripe:

I am the sole survivor of my former ship, on which I served as chaplain. The men onboard this vessel were shipping prisoners, who were travelling in chains; we journeyed for months until a storm besieged us. The lumber could not withstand the weight of the waves, and all men, both elites and peasants, were thrown overboard and drowned. With no one steering the ship, she was vulnerable to the wind, yet, with a bit of luck, the ship transported me to land. I'm afraid history has repeated itself with the arrival of this second vessel, yet this instance had spared these criminals.

As he finished these last according words, teefer absorbed and digested; it was as if the story was relevant only for a moment. It relieved the curiosity, yet, once closure was reached, it was no longer important: *I'll have time to think while their minds be dormant.*

The sleeves of Prize were pried open and Aces of all suits fell into the Ocean. There lay the Jack of Spades, which landed on teefer's face, signifying his own rank and grave for that of Mr Trade. And the nine of diamonds shall be claimed by Pope John the eighth, disguised to narrate. As for the Blade, he be the ten of Staves, with him being lower rank in spite of how they behaved. A pair of sevens were laid out for the Twins, and, for Blay and Thatcher, six and nine pips. A black-and-white Joker whistled through the wind, while the Jack of Hearts circled and spinned. Then two final cards were laid out for Prize and Robin; they be the Ace of Hearts and their King. But since all fours had already been drawn, it was clear from the start that Prize's Ace was a fraud. And all could see clearly who Prize really was: he be the coloured Joker, waitin' for your applause.

Prize was exposed, and his anger was shown in the act of grinding his teeth, shattering his golden molars and displaying the rotters beneath. As his pride was surely lost, his world went into chaos. He lost the curve and lost his nerve. He was no longer a charmer and no longer superb. There were no thoughts of consequence, though he be bleedin' from the teeth. He was grindin' his gums, mashing them to bloody meat. The confrontation was too verbose, and his desperation had juxtaposed his cloak. He became broken without a method to excuse his decrepit abuse. Openly ignoring this bungle, he ran cowardly into the jungle. With all the pride stripped away, Robin, childe and teefer were now the same.

The storm had subsided, so teefer decided to instruct the remaining misguided to craft a small raft. Flotsam was collected once more, like when teefer had explored the first beach of bottled draft. Only, this time, he omitted his shame, his pride, his sin, and his craving for wine and juniper gin. 'Twas because all the flawed had either left or died. First, there was Blay, who'd brought the shame; once he wrote that letter, pride made its claim. Then there be the fool who'd had too much to drink. His end would yield the ability to think. There were the twins who opposed each other; destruction and creation are what represented these brothers. Mr Thatcher was next – another flavour of pride. He reflected machismo, the most cumbersome of lies. Then there be the Blade, who'd often retaliate; he was marooned for the way he behaved. Finally, there was Prize, the most recent to depart; he acted his part by playing with your heart. And, since all sins were clear, what remained was wisdom and childhood fear. Regarding this, the Robin had told all, explaining his role in this mindscape of Jack Trade's soul.

♠ ♣ ♥ ♦

Soon, the three had built a barge, so that they could discover, by and large, the deepest intertwined secrets to locate the black beach to see what they might find. But, unfortunately for John, fate delayed for too long, and the secrets once revealed died in the wake of this song. You see, when accrued pride is consumed it is assumed that it will eventually resume. This casts doubt on the route to redemption, as the devil always returns to scout the situation.

The smell of a disease came flowing through the breeze. A smell of rotten teeth impeded the belief of the remaining three. Chiefly and proud, pride reaches around to surround the crowd like a scud cloud. Shuffling into the liquid, the three were now afloat and drifting. Black clouds of cognitive doubt had risen from two competing crowds. Let us now acknowledge that each time we abolish the trait of any nasty sort, a storm arises that signifies the crashing of the wise in our thoughts. A lightning bolt strikes nearby, derived from abandoned pride. While childe hides behind his allies, Robin guides teefer to protect their lives. And soon they elude this feud by excluding the attitude of the aforementioned few who were drinking teefer's brew.

To question me is to question with doubt. A ruthless opinion is an answer without, and, loudly, a cry comes pouring out. *For years, you've been drinking your stout. And, now that you've found out, you can no longer hide this lie. An evil so feeble, 'tis not worth your time. I hope you choose to speak truths this line, now that you've been told about the greatest lie.*

Educated by the old and wise, teefer begged for understanding, though heaven knows why. He understood his words, as he'd seen and heard all. But, without lips to speak, he was forever in duel. Yet, now that the wise had given him freedom, he would begin to listen and understand who's been cheating. That would be all he said before Robin is transferred to the dead in a single thread. Those were the last words from this man's deathbed.

In the blink of an eye, from green to grey, colours blend to shades and fade away as we age. And so Robin, the Old Wise Man dies. Care to try, dare to cry. Hope to witness those things in mind with his own two eyes. The things he recognized are no longer the issues he despised and no longer will the hunger come crashing through with denial. And of course, for all of those days, Robin's teeth were not so pretty. Replaced with wooden chips over years of self-pity. Once his maw was filled with pearly whites, but they'd been lost over time from all those lonely nights.

The corpse was sewn into his clothes and thrown into the water, sinking like a stone. Appearing within the atmospheric zone there came each and every colour of a full circle rainbow. As the storm had bled that final drop of rain, no more would Teefer drink a glass of champagne, all for the sake of his own damn health. A man may fool all that he is someone else, but he can never fool himself.

Shanty xix

♥

The Reliable Narrator

AVOID REFLECTING ON ONESELF DEVIATES, FORCING OTHERS TO self-reflect, which compensates. Attacking that group for their differences, so subtly. The next town over or the next-door neighbour – whichever the area, one needs an enemy. It's banter, it's in the culture, it's a game of abuse. It's how you dish it out and take it that decides whether you win or lose. You must join in the suffering, you must learn to play, else you may become bullied and feel rather betrayed. So join in with the quick thinkers; they've all adapted, and today is their day.

We'd threaten to leave, but we'd already left. Escape from this island and now you escape the crime of theft. We'd left once, but we'd longed for our traditions. Yet, when we returned, we resented that decision. 'Twas but the contradiction of leaving our home, that be Great

Britain, for the King and throne. So we retained the right to withstand the fight. The London pride we shall never hide, despite the challenges and despite the classes being unbalanced. We love our land, no matter how damaged. Don't be concerned with this at all; we'll manage. Like the pig that craves the mud or the soldier and his lust for blood, we'll continue to roll around in squalor, while the elite yank that slave's collar.

And who be the elite to see, but Daniel Foe to visit thee. Known for his stories about piracy and adventures on the open seas.

Who is the reliable narrator? He asks us, but we don't want to make a fuss, so this we simply neglect to discuss, and thus he must gain our trust with an opening offer. At first, we do nothing to bother, but the notion that we been written about for the commoners to hear brings this to our attention and so we lend him an ear.

There be John; we all call him 'Teefer', for his particular epithet most suits his grotesque nature. How can he be the voice? He ain't got no choice; he ain't the one 'ere to be rejoiced. But, then again, we started with him. He be drinkin' Ocean water, thinkin' it be gin. Per'aps that be Edif, she be writing it all down; she be stood by idly watchin' all them thieving clowns. Edif O'Neal be the neutral party, without the flaw of emotion, while the rest of the cunts chucked it straight into the Ocean. But she ain't omnipotent, not like God; perhaps He'd be the one to whom we'd bettin' all the odds. And then there is in fact 'me', spewing out all my history to use them bastards to bolster my needs. Then there's 'we', that be Jack. We all acknowledge the man with the knife in his back.

We'd be God of our own salty earth by now, since childhood, if not all the way since our birth. Marked with an asymmetrical face: one side stricken with pain, while the other shows guile and a smile. There you see a multitude of conflicting personas. Never mind, they'll be there for a while, until that rope ties round our neck, squeezing the breath out from our chest. This will be the defining moment; this will be the genesis of our shattered components. A life after this – an afterlife, that is – truly, in this we believe. We may conceive the end with a mixture of reality and fantasy, so that we may live in infamy for eternity. And this Daniel Foe offers an alternative method to remain in the minds of the neglected and accepted.

So let that revolution proceed, and let my story continue to feed those starving souls with no once of hope; so it may reach the lower and the upper, and the ears of the Pope. Let's bang on the doors of the exclusives and throw bricks right through their windows. Ransack the rooms for trinkets of value; those items undeserved with their biased worldview. Set fire to their gardens, tear down their statues, vandalize their mansions, rip up their flag and obstruct their expansion. Tear down the walls of expectation. Shovel salt in the cracks of the skin and soil; starve the land of its gold and oil. Stealing Nature's essence, as one alchemist attempts. This is the taste of greed that we all know best.

Searching for the path triggers that memory of a longing moment long forgotten. So you dream of the rotten without dealing with the truth: that the child had been beaten, withstanding his abuse. One carves the world around oneself to perpetuate the lie, that his hero shielding the fear is one impeccable guy. Confidence is the charade – 'tis the lie. 'Tis for the audience or those who believe; only for them, but not I. For I am the only one who holds the facts, yet I buried these details for the sanity of Jack. For I've been the core of this journey all along, I've been the centre of it all. They be the weak; I be the strong. Fear is the foundation of a multitude of pride, those features used to protect the little boy who hides.

I'll write it down expressively, from the pulp in raw form. To the core you've impressed me like to the heart of a whore. They chose to adore while I chose to record this gibberish you spiral, the commoners will love you for decades and a while. Knock 'em down to get their attention one way or another; you try to offend them. You've got much more to hide in your lies than mine, so I'll read between the lines. After your death, I'll down that glass of gin and pray. I'll write it all down for you while your body will lay. This is my last encounter, Mr Trade; perhaps I'll see you again. Farewell to you; I'll pray for your soul and archive your life, my friend.

Shanty xx

◆

"Through Thick and Thin"

T HE MANIPULATION BEGINS WITH A STATEMENT. HE SETS THEM up, as the rest lead the way. Small talk develops into dialogue, and soon the men become acquainted. He shares little knowledge, as they share all. He conceals his identity, as they have yet to entail. Not by vague conversions but also not in detail. The faces of villain are immediately entertained, yet the remnants of the gentlemen are left to face the shame.

As Teefer put all his cards on the table, he felt slightly insecure. Teefer felt the walls caving in, although he wasn't particularly sure. With one subtle remark at a time, in no doubt about Teefer's mind, Prize continued to win them over, pushing his luck in the rhyme. The time for lying was over. Teefer took his hat from his sweaty head and plopped it on the table, adjacent to his cards. Cracks from the Paris beau had breathed out their last. Through the removal of his stealth, Teefer exposed his naked self. His sword was now unsheathed, as he showed a smile of crooked, rotten teeth.

Highest trump out, lowest trump out, Jack of Spades and Game: each trick worth one point, which therefore was the aim.

Not so fast, mate; you've got three black Jacks here, said Prize with a cunning sneer. Teefer could have sworn the third Jack was red.

You must have slipped that card in, Teefer boldly said. The accusations had begun with a smile on Prize's figure, described as malevolent, with a cheap and nasty snigger.

The master rules by eyeing his slave, and neither man wanted to surrender this game. Prize was more experienced in this way; by leading Teefer to break, he would soon cave. This triggered a violence in Teefer and, without wisdom, a brawl began. Punches and kicks were thrown all round, between a demon and a man. A bottle is smashed from Prize's bloody hands and lunges for the dirty neck of his chief captain. With a swift dodge to the right, Teefer reclaimed control of the fight and smothered the bastard with two hands of sleight.

Rage flowed out like atrophied lightning that shatters and scatters the colours in the sky, sending a chain reaction to Teefer's emotions and projecting each colour on the man's face in an instant. His eyes mumbled a stern frown, and, subtly, his facial muscles formed a hysterical smile; not the smirk of a child, but that of a madman.

Flesh composed of ornate meat, supported with bone and rope secured by the cleat. Pressure from the thumbs pushed into the throat; pull tight the rope to secure the gunboat. Strength was used to lift those crates of freight, with a touch of hate the blood could no longer circulate. Blood vessels in the eyes widened in size; pressure from opposing winds caused sails to diverge. Apply more pressure and the sail will surely rip; with more force from the fingernails and the vessels soon burst.

♠ ♣ ♥ ♦

Face the blue sky for a while, now that the deed has been done. *Sit with me, young Childe. Keep me company under the sun.* He patted him on the head, as if he were his own son, and asked the boy for his name; thus, the truth had begun. Yet the boy did not comply; he was without speech, yet not for the same reason why Old Man could not speak. Childe did not feel safe with Teefer's contempt; in the past, he had no say in front of these corrupt men. Now that they had gone, Childe freely displayed that he was afraid. This was his first chance to get up and run away. Teefer wanted to confide in Childe and to confess his sins in this exile. Teefer chased the boy, so that he could face his final trial.

Shanty XXI

♠

"Between the Devil and the Deep, Blue Sea"

ND THEN WE COME TO THAT FINAL ISLAND, THE BLACK BEACH AS PROMISED, SO chin up and smile. Crunchy, volcanic dust, as rough as crystallized sand, left black soot upon Teefer's feet and hands as he crawled on all fours; he be weepin' without brew, for he be nowhere without the members of his crew. So there he returned, like a maggot in the dirt, crawlin' around to quench his thirst. He crawled on the floor in search of a drop of the ol' pure, suckin' on the ground but nothing there can be found. The mind applies the crudest method to sustain its energy; 'tis why Teefer reacted in desperate need on this island of Tahiti. But not for attention; that be from the alcohol. So there he went on his routine pub crawl.

He crawled through the crashing sea to approach the black sand. He knew the beach like the back of his father's hand. Prepared for the darkness as he eyes the night. Waiting for dusk as his hair turns white. Rummage through the dirt like beasts in the Wilde, find your treasure in the buried sand, and live freedom for a while. Each of these missing personas is like part of a castle. Each field of interest's like a tower, with the final touches to his spire, his significant other, his bruised-eyed lover. But when the towers come crashing down in deepest dread; he found himself lost in a chasm, his fear now becoming and his faith in spasm.

And just then did Childe appear with tears, to which Teefer had no choice but to lend him an ear. He searched all pockets for the lad to soothe. He opened his hands revealing an almost empty bottle of booze.

Here ya go. Drink this! instructed Teefer. Yet the boy's tears melted in the bottle of ether. *A man doesn't cry, he drinks 'till the pain stops. That's how one becomes the man on top. Consume it like those tears in the tankard. Then you'll see how to fuel your anger.*

With no words to offer, yet capable of communication, Childe substituted speech with gesture and, consequently, narration. Childe pointed Teefer to stare into a puddle, in which Teefer witnessed a baby being cuddled. Teefer peered closer as he saw a figment of himself as the infant loved by all in an instant. Another scene emerged and the black puddle revealed a young Jack Trade playing in the field. A father approached, showing love and affection, leaving Teefer with more than just a question.

Exemplified by chilling stories, the little blighter who'd learnt to dream of a life worth living, sought a life by the stern. Creating his own characters in a story of his own, he dreamed of being the King of England, with his crown and throne. Other pleasantries arrived in this stream of visions, and, in search of these discoveries, he remembered all that was missing. Yet, in search of this, some pain around his scruff wrapped around it like a snake and took him back to his bluff. Developed beyond his capabilities only to throw it all away on the death of his father, the young Jack Sheppard disobeyed.

He waited for an unknown source. And, in the course of his ponder, he remembered the root of the pain in his collar. That he be strangled with a noose; around his neck did dwell, witnessed by all, his audience cheered his descent to Hell. This was one of many hidden messages on this timeless voyage awaiting Teefer's discovery, despite his impending annoyance. For he was reluctant to face his spoilage and the disloyalty of those who followed. Teefer was expecting coinage, thus reliving his borrows. A flashback for Jack occurred, which would stir and mix his memories to fix his method of thinking. A clearer image of Jack should have surfaced of his whoring around and excessive drinking. Produced was a riled remembrance of his nemesis; that be Jonathan Wilde and his supported arrogance.

There he was, left with a simple choice to accept his death or retain his voice. Acceptance would have been the submissive path; though it was unknown what his decision would be. Or he could have taken the Devil's route and continued to dominate the story. What would occur in the next shanty would merely be mystery; a collection of fantasies based on the denial of me, that be Childe who could not speak freely. *Let that be the way that Teefer chooses, to remain in this place to maintain the ruse. Let Teefer's time be frozen; let that be the path that Teefer has chosen.*

And it was here that he be greetin' all of his chums; they include Solomon Blay, who'd been rather glum. But who could blame the cunt who hadn't touched Teefer's rum? So there Teefer went to pour him a glass; he put his arm around Blay, who now served as upper class. Then appeared Sod, for he was still rather greasy; he'd sing a tune or two, despite how sleazy. Teefer, inspired by Sod's courage downed with him a drop of gin and blackcurrant. Then appeared Guido and Gulliver, with their destructive and constructive ways; Teefer placed a hand on each's shoulder, and a grin appeared on his face. Then there be the Goliath of a man with all of Jack's hate. Teefer posed a fake punch to the man with all that weight. Suddenly, appeared his mistake, which came through Bill Blyth, who he'd recently betrayed. No apologies were necessary, put all quarrels aside; they buried the hatchet, and all was forgiven for Teefer and the Knife. And, finally, came Prize with all the tricks up his sleeve, surprising all them punters he'd deceived and whose attention he'd achieved.

'Twas as if no blood had been spilt and no shame had been faced, with no contemplation of guilt. A few laughs here and a few drinks to slake, and all the lads became the closest mates, except old man and childe, who both became silent and whose names remained in lower case. And, in his afterlife, Teefer and his crew continued to live the fantasy, oblivious to Jack's issues. But I still be here writing down the flow; I be the ship's chief clerk 'Edif O'Neal', also known as Daniel Foe.

Shanty XXII

♣

Execution
"The Bitter End"

Y OU SPEND YOUR WHOLE LIFE TRYING TO BE THE Prize, AND
it can take all eternity to tell you otherwise. When
men die or disappear, Teefer is left with nostalgia and
fear. 'Twas the mix of two emotions combined, through
a life derived in that childe's mind. You thought the
foundation was selfish pride, but, the truth be told, pride
sits on its hind. Arrogance covers its ignorant ears and
suppresses those tears, but, all along, the true foundation
was forgotten fears.

Thou put that noose round me nape or abide by the
Bloody Code. We were up to our ears in piss 'n' moan,
but we'll never render or surrender to the throne. We

reject your United Kingdom, for we got our bloody own. Curse me wide at arm full. It became very clear that they made us into an example. They threw the book at us – an old, crumpled Bible. The gospel left no stain on my soul, since God was still the rival. And, in spite of it all, we be grinning; we be pleased. We have our audience finally; we have them begging on their knees.

So will it be a beheading or a burning at the stake? Will we be gone like Blackbeard, Guy Fawkes or perhaps Sir Francis Drake? Soon all the questions will be answered, and our moment shall be. England will never more rain on our dignity. The grinning face fills up the midnight sky, and, when the misery comes in broad daylight, the faced-filled laughs will turn to cries. Them children had no idea of the men's complaints. Nor did they learn to give an ear to them severe constraints. So, no care came from that. As a matter of fact, as the years went on, they never dared to shed those tears and cry over the bloody meat, butchered right here on the main street. In the market, they be hanging on the butcher's hook, so that all may take a look at the severed heads, all displayed to be placed on our dinner plate. And I can tell you what, mate; it ain't no pretty place. 'Tis where all the horror occurs. 'Tis where me noggin infers where me own execution will be held. The end of my time on Earth and the beginning of my own Hell.

Looking up from the box in the dirt. I see them all dressed in black and hurt. So we told them the Gov'nor wanted us dead. *Tie a rope around his neck*, they said. *Sever the body from the head, and let's all watch his legs twitch at the end.* Such a cruel bastard this bloke, as we stand there holding our composure, but there's no need to convince the people, for they commemorate our exposure. The show was all for us; we've nothing to hide. As long as we're still alive, we'll display our infamy with ego and pride. The crowd'll never judge our name, defame it in shame, you'll bet. We shall wear our name tag proudly, with chin pointing towards the sunset. And with the whole world watching, we'll never look back. The audience will want you more, so restrain, remain and retain yourself, Jack.

As we age with this burden, the force of this mind becomes heavier, and soon we discover we will never recover. A golden age, in those glory days; that be the man who would have been old and grey. Through an abstract maze, he makes his own way through a thickened haze; chasing himself to oblivion, he reflects on his past mistakes. He soon will capture that glorious rapture, within his own madness still fractured, expressed across these chapters.

So we reject that fate and take our place in the noose, sealing our legacy, which we'll never lose. Rhyming slang by the bard, a street preacher, a misdemeanour spoken in tongues. The crowd gathers round to that laudable one. Hanging there with all eyes to see, with a grin on my face, so the crowd cheers for me. So here we go to death we smile and all we see now is white light and then silence for a while.

AFTERWORD

♥

A RECURRENT THEME IN THIS NOVEL IS THAT PRIDE TENDS TO have priority over psychological well-being and physical health. This notion is exemplified by an unreliable narrator (the stranger / John Teefer), who consumes seawater from empty bottles floating along the shoreline, which are assumed to be filled with alcohol. The novel is divided into two stories: themes plaguing the life of Jack Trade as he awaits his execution, and a fantastical series of events that occur during the afterlife of Jack Trade. This latter part makes up the bulk of the novella, and symbolizes Jack's thoughts and behaviours in the former, expressed as monologue. Within this novella, Jack Trade summons his own reality, composed of a role and identity he has lived and fooled himself to believe. The two stories are merged finally in the last 'shanty', in which the monologue of Jack Trade and the resolution of Jack's consciousness occurs during his execution. This merging represents Jack's acknowledgement of reality and fantasy as a continuum; i.e. his afterlife.

The story often references "the secrets of her" or "hidden messages of the Ocean". These refer to representations of the subconscious – the underlying foundation of Trade's mindscape. In addition, the references to nature in general (e.g. white beach, black beach, jungle and storm) are pointing towards the subconscious, while the characters point towards the conscious. The persona of Teefer is the main character of the latter story, who reflects Jack Trade's ability to manipulate his own subconscious. "Consuming her secrets" refers to the abrupt and failed attempt to bridge the conscious and subconscious states. The sea has a natural course, and pride keeps us against the flow of its current.

The theory I posit is that one develops multiple selves throughout the duration of one's life, yet it originates with the child self. During this development, the mind creates its own internal audience, which is exemplified as Trade's crew members. This audience can be an entity who watches us, secures us and gives us a reason to strive towards the identities whom we try to aspire to become, irrespective of the potential conflicts between our child self and our aspiring selves.

Another theme of the story is associated with the struggle between the ego and God. A secular person who does not attribute their insecurities to a higher power substitutes this higher power in the form of inflated pride. Essentially, God serving as the internal audience who witnesses and judges our behaviour is replaced with an inflated ego manifested by the selves one develops throughout the duration of one's life. This implies that non-secular thinking involves playing the role of one's own God, by judging one's own behaviour, asserting morality and satisfying the internal audience by occasionally bolstering the ego. With success, the internal audience will applaud for its own actions. However, when the inner audience and the external audience conflict with one another, the ego is offended. This notion is expressed using cognitive dissonance theory from several characters throughout the story.

Asymmetry is another recurrent theme in the story, reflecting specifically the idea that trauma and pain causes the face to become asymmetric, representing sorrow and anger on the left and right side, respectively. Some examples include; "A conflict is posed to the man of the external, while the other man inside writes it down in his journal"; "one eye fixated on this savage band, the other eye tells the story of a boy becoming a man"; "causal pain can leave asymmetric cracks on the face, accumulated from a lifetime of harsh constraint"; and "marked with an asymmetrical face; one side stricken with pain, while the other shows guile and a smile". The notion here is that all faces are asymmetrical to some degree, which reflects different aspects of one's personality. The more trauma in a person's life, the more asymmetry is expressed.

Each character Teefer greets is a persona of Jack Trade. Jack Trade's true self is Childe, who is motivated by the fear of losing his innocence. The presumed goal of Childe is to mature to the wise and humble person reflected in Old Man, though both personas are suppressed by Teefer's stronger personas (Prize, Bill the Knife, Thatcher, Guido, Gulliver and Sod). Solomon Blay is the weakest persona, representing depression and despair. With the exception of Teefer and Prize, all characters are either based on either characters in other published stories or real-life notorious people who existed between the 1600s and 1800s. These characters are meant to reflect Jack Trade's idols/heroes, who juxtapose with the path of villainy he praises and aspires to.

Another symbolic image that reflects disdain is the butchering of meat; when butchering a pig within a butcher's shop, how it is displayed in the open and without remorse for the animal is similar to a public execution. Hence, the public display of butchering an animal is analogous to the butchering of a criminal.

NOTES ON CHARACTERS

◆

THE EVENTS OF JACK TRADE ARE LOOSELY BASED ON THE CELEBRITY THIEF, JACK Sheppard; hence the subtle reference to 'Sheppard' in Shanty 21. Many of the events mentioned throughout the story occur after Sheppard's death (1724): the industrial age, from 1760–1820; the penal colonization of Australia from 1788–1868. In addition, the painting "Black-eyed Sue and Sweet Poll of Plymouth taking leave of their lovers who are going to Botany Bay", by Robert Sayer in 1792 was also a source of inspiration for this novel, specifically for the character Black-eyed Sally. The name was changed for rhyming purposes. With the exception of Robinson Crusoe by Daniel Defoe in 1719, the other references used occur after Jack Sheppard's death: 'London' by William Blake in 1794, *Treasure Island* by Robert Louis Stevenson in 1883, and *Gulliver's Travels* by Jonathon Swift in 1726.

Guido reflects Guido Fawkes, infamously involved in the Gunpowder Plot of 5th November, 1605. His character revolves around the plan to seek revenge on elites, who are seen by Jack as supreme manipulators. His twin is portrayed as Lemuel Gulliver from the novel *Gulliver's Travels* by Jonathan Swift (1726). The only character to be based on fictional work is Gulliver, who represents artisanry and heroism, and who juxtaposes with Trade's true intentions. Edward Thatcher has been cited as the birth name of the infamous pirate Blackbeard, who was an active pirate between 1716 and 1718. Bill 'The Knife' Blyth is loosely based on William Bligh (1754–1817) who was ironically betrayed in the mutiny on *HMS Bounty*. Solomon Blay is based on an English convict who later become an executioner in Australia during the latter half of the nineteenth century. Teefer, Prize and Sod are fictional characters. 'Prize' is a term used in naval conflicts to refer to a captured vessel. 'Sod' is British slang for an unpleasant man, though the word also has other meanings. 'Teefer' is a cryptonym for thief.

The name Teefer also refers to the grotesque teeth of the protagonist, which portray his image symbolically, as well as other different aspects of each character. The teeth of Teefer are crooked, reflecting his imperfection. Behind this lavish golden façade, we discover that Prize's rotten teeth are no better than Teefer's in that respect. Old man is revealed to have wooden teeth, or eighteenth-century dentures. Sod could sing a tune or two, so, naturally, he had a whistle as he had a large gap between his two front teeth. Without hope, Blay loses all his teeth from scurvy, which reflects Jack's guilt for ignoring his faith. "Bill the Knife would smile to your face while he'd be sleeping with your wife", indicative of his deed of betrayal. Guido's destructive manner is portrayed by grinding his teeth when his right leg is being sawn by Thatcher, who has no mention of his teeth since he is 'already dignified'. Gulliver has perfect, white teeth, as he portrays the only hero of the story; his heroic deeds are ignored by the rest of the crew, representing different masks of personification of pride and villainy.

Narration is often played with for multiple purposes. The narrative point of view told by Jack Trade is in first person perspective, yet altered to conform to contemporary working-class British speech; replacing 'I', 'me', or 'mine' to 'we', 'us' or 'ours' as a way of persuading other people to be involved in an event. For example, a person asking for a drink at the local pub can ask, "Will you buy me a pint?" or perhaps more authentically "Will you buy *us* a pint?" The narrative point of view is also used as a device to allow the reader as to assume the role of one of Jack's personas. The narrative voice is also a key element to the story, as is evidenced in Shanty 19 The Reliable Narrator. In the perspective of John Teefer (narrated by Edif O'Neal), all characters assume the role of the narrator at one point or another, yet are all unreliable narrators. Only one narrator is reliable. In Shanty 19, the true narrator is revealed to be Daniel Defoe (referred to in the novel as Foe). Edif O'Neal is an anagram of Daniel Foe, hence Teefer's story is told by Daniel Foe, yet disguised as a character in the story. In reality, Daniel DeFoe visited and wrote about Jack Sheppard and Jonathan Wilde while they awaited execution in early eighteenth century, London.